Rilke in Paris

Rilke in Paris

Rainer Maria Rilke and Maurice Betz

Translated by Will Stone

Published by Hesperus Press Limited
28 Mortimer Street, London W1W 7RD
www.hesperuspress.com

This translation first published by Hesperus Press Limited, 2012
Translation © Will Stone, 2012

Designed and typeset by Fraser Muggeridge studio
Printed in Jordan by Jordan National Press

ISBN: 978-1-84391-369-6

Contents

Translator's Introduction

'I sense that to work is to live without dying…'
RMR

Rainer Maria Rilke arrived in Paris for the first time on 28 August, 1902, as a still youthful poet seeking the best experiences and location from which to access his inwardness, a poet whose body of work, though already receiving recognition, had not yet earned its distinction of genius. He left it for the last time in the same month twenty-three years later, a celebrated poetic figure in poor health, whose legacy was now confirmed. The following year, in 1926, he died at his home, at the chateau of Muzot in the Valais, a French-speaking canton of Switzerland. During those twenty-four intervening years the French capital would become for Rilke, a poet who, more than any other, oiled his precarious existence with almost continual European

1. The gardens of the Palais Royal

peregrination and a heavy dose of patronage, the place he might call home. However, in the midst of these two decades of ever-penurious creative germination, sprouting, blossoming and harvest, crouched the black dog of the First World War. Despite his relatively benign experience of war (three months of military service in Vienna), the 1914–18 conflict constituted an external trauma that threatened to usurp Rilke's mental cartography, leaving him drained and disorientated in terms of his ability to continue his literary work. He was forced back to Germany for the duration of the conflict and the severing from his previous life of European displacement, together with a sense of horror at the war's catastrophic annihilating power, the ruthless removal of both individual personalities and the creatively rich era that produced them, ushered in a period of sterility, which was only resolved long after the war's end.

Having dispensed with overbearing family ties and fled the perceived provincialism of Prague, Rilke was a hypersensitive dreamer adrift, nurturing a growing pregnancy of the senses. But to deliver the birth and be relieved of this weight, to coax his latent talent to manifest itself properly, he needed an atmosphere that was sympathetic to his complex and not yet fully marshalled inner self; a precise location equipped to sustain such an undertaking. He was also looking for a personal master, a senior example from whom he could take counsel, whose behavior he might replicate to bring on those inner shoots he increasingly realized must not bloom prematurely, if they were to achieve anything of lasting greatness. From those first feelers in Paris at the dawn of the century, until final salvation in a veritable 'storm of creativity', at Muzot in 1922, all Rilke's movements and behaviour, his aspirations and energies, are focused on this sole requirement for inner synthesis. It is this unremitting search with its dead ends and disappointments, its sudden unforeseen deliverances and mysterious gifts, that Betz traverses so poignantly in his essay, quoting liberally from the copious and notably rich letters penned by the poet to his wife and friends and from *The Notebooks of Malte Laurids Brigge*, the now famous prose work that consummates Rilke's Paris experience.

Touring Russia with Lou Andreas-Salomé in 1900, Rilke thought he might find a guiding figure in the great novelist Tolstoy. But to no avail. (See 'Notes on Places'.) Rilke appealed to Tolstoy for counsel:

> I still lack the discipline, the being able to work and the being compelled to work, for which I have longed for years. Do I lack the strength? Is my will sick? It is the dream in me that hinders all action? Days go by and sometimes I hear life passing. And still nothing has happened. Still there is nothing real about me.

Tolstoy's answer was simply 'write!', but Rilke, having come such a great distance, was hoping for a few more words of wisdom. He moved on to the artists' colony of Worpswede, amid the wind-combed heaths and plains of Northern Germany. Another potential location perhaps, but through those he befriended, and, in the case of the young sculptor Clara Westhoff, married, he only edged closer to the defining figure of Rodin and the unknown quantity of Paris. By the close of summer 1902, he was finally in the capital, meeting the great artist, and here his relationship with France properly begins.

France, traditionally viewed as the natural home of the artist, still professed in Rilke's day at least, to sustain an 'aristocracy of talent'. Here it was thought genius could best flourish, the ideal of beauty, 'le beau', still endured right down to the common man, and the artist was seen as the necessary foil to the spiritual paralysis of the bourgeois or philistine. And although Austrian writer Rudolf Kassner warned that Rilke's love for France was 'nothing more than the German love for the foreign', it is obvious that, even in the first flush of his relationship, France offered Rilke the pertinent literary and artistic architecture to coincide with his precociously maturing tastes and appetite for a concentrated cultural education. While based in Paris he made many instructive trips to the provinces. He visited the Roman ruins of Provence, the medieval towns of Burgundy, the cathedrals of Chartres, Bourges, Reims and many other notable locations. France provided the great personal examples of the patient indefatigable worker, from Rodin, who figures so strongly in the early period and in the pages of *Rilke in Paris*, through to Cézanne, interpreted as such through his biography and then in the later period in Paris, the Franco-Belgian poet Emile Verhaeren. Rilke who had roused the ghost of Verhaeren as 'Mr V' in his controversial 'Worker's Letter' of 1922, revered the Belgian poet as a visionary master 'of the here and now'. Rilke was rarely without a collection of Verhaeren to hand in this period and constantly expounds on the life-affirming breadth and energy of his poetry, especially that of the post-humously published *Les Flammes Hautes* of 1917, in letters to friends and patrons.

2. The Panthéon from the Luxembourg Gardens

In Maurice Betz, France also offered a sympathetic and dedicated translator of Rilke's works, and during that last summer in Paris the two worked closely on the French translation of *The Notebooks of Malte Laurids Brigge*, the work that forms the backbone of *Rilke in Paris*. In fact it is evident that, along with Italy in a supporting role, France and French culture are the dominant guiding forces of Rilke's adult life, exemplified perhaps by the fact that he celebrated this relationship by writing some four hundred poems in French, translated a clutch of French poets, chose to settle in a French-speaking region and became, in his later years, more deeply absorbed in the work of the French poet Paul Valéry than in that of any other writer. In the Valais Rilke claimed that he had found a combination of landscape and climate more perfect than any other he had encountered during his life. For even then, the search was no less pressing to find the ideal productive climate, the location and atmosphere most conducive to unbroken solitude and steady unhindered work.

However, not all was straightforward or comfortable for Rilke during his final sojourn in Paris, and Betz provides some hints at the close of his essay on the rather ambiguous and not always fulfilling relationships Rilke experienced in his involvement with the Parisian literary scene. Betz also suggests that the sometimes vague and nonchalant Valéry did not always give Rilke the level of attention that the latter would have liked. However, the curious bond between these two very different poets was one of respectful mutual awareness of their significance, and a realisation of what each one might gain from the other. But crucially only Rilke had the measure of the other's language. Valéry struggled to gain a foothold in Rilke's mysterious universe of feelings, while Rilke was intoxicated by the French poet's condensed language, his way of getting to the core with the minimum of fuss. Rilke felt he was always on the back foot by being obliged to express himself in German. He saw in Valéry a clear path through the thicket to the light-filled glade beyond, and through his free translations of the poetry determined to follow it. But Valéry, analytical, methodical, intellectual, was the antipode to Rilke's romantic, subjective poetry of feeling. Rilke excitedly discovered in Valéry's French the kind of language vehicle he himself had been trying to design from German for years, and whose blueprint Valéry, now emerging suddenly into the light, calmly and confidently laid down like a Royal Flush. Rilke was drawn into a profound seduction, where the seducer was never quite able to reciprocate.

Furthermore, despite the sterling support of Gide, who had translated some of the *Notebooks* and overseen his transition into French, Rilke suffered a certain disillusionment during his final period in Paris, worn out by the endless round of superficial social gatherings and introductions, which seemed to have sprouted from nowhere and threatened to suffocate his precious time in the city. As Betz reminds us, Rilke had written on fame in his book on Rodin, describing it as 'the collection of misunderstandings that gather around a name' and it seems this was borne out to some degree during his last eight months in Paris. Rilke seemed in some sense to be an anachronism in the Paris of the twenties. There is an intriguing incident recounted by Stefan Zweig in his memoirs, of Rilke attending a function and entering into a monologue whose depth and sensitivity, perhaps too onerous for the occasion, served only to alienate the other guests, who one by one walked awkwardly away, leaving the poet virtually addressing himself, an alienated solitary figure. Zweig also recounts an earlier sighting of Rilke, when he chanced upon the poet riding the top deck of an omnibus, as if in a trance, curiously out of place amongst the other passengers. The sight of Rilke awkwardly embedded in this modern vehicle, silently passing in anonymity and unaware of his friend's presence, had clearly touched Zweig.

Since everything and everyone he encountered could potentially be of service to his artistic development, and since his life was in the most explicit sense an ongoing 'journey', which required its journeyman to be unencumbered and agile, Rilke has inadvertently left himself open to criticism of a certain 'ruthlessness' towards those he seduced, drew earnestly into his orbit and then as quickly abandoned. This was exacerbated perhaps by his failure to maintain any semblance of a normal family life. Rilke had always been eclectic in his choices to say the least, and as in other areas of his life, there is the feeling that many of those he drew towards him, or whose confidence he gained, were there to be donors for whatever they could contribute to his art and then to be jettisoned like husks after their fruit had been garnered. K.A.J Batterby in the book *Rilke and France* (Oxford, 1966), summarises this trend.

> In general Rilke's contacts with artistic figures have the character of a series of separate and sometimes apparently unrelated episodes. As soon as their purpose was fulfilled they ceased. When Rilke had exhausted all their possibilities and assimilated all he could from them, they were discarded. Rilke's progress resembles a series of distinct scaling operations, after each of which the ladder was kicked away. That is not to say that he forgot those associations, and certainly he never lost what he gained from them; but they were never allowed to outlive their usefulness.

The war years, when Rilke was forced away from France, gave him the opportunity to contemplate Paris and its importance to his poetic development as Batterby puts it 'in absentia protracta'. The sudden wrench of leaving Paris had been costly, in both mental and material terms. All Rilke's belongings were simply left behind in his compartment in the rue Campagne-Première studio and then sold off in his absence. This must have felt like an inglorious and shabby end to his Paris residence and in a sense it was, for although he returned to the city on two more occasions, one very brief lasting only six days in 1920 and then again for a period of seven months in 1925, he was never to re-establish that sense of continuity and the settled periods of fruitful labour that he had experienced before the war.

3. St Sulpice at night

Between 1902 and 1914, Paris was the proverbial magnet that always drew Rilke back from his restless wanderings, whether in Italy, Scandinavia, Belgium, Germany or Spain. One only has to glance at the interweaving addresses of his Paris residencies to get some idea of the resilience and intricacy of this relationship. Paris both fundamentally oppressed Rilke, compelling him to depart elsewhere, and summoned him back with a kind of nostalgic urgency, which he was unable to resist. For Rilke, Paris gradually became the guardian of the productive stretches of elusive solitude he constantly sought. Paris flaunted the overarching magnificence of its past and enduring physical beauty, whilst at the same time trailing indifferently in its wake the gruesome reality of an abandoned caste of society existing hand to mouth on its streets. The city, bloated with unacknowledged suffering and a vortex of futile energies, both repelled and enthralled him. Though entranced by its legendary architecture and art, the perspectives and vistas, the parks and gardens, the wealth of churches and hidden convents, Rilke was always chased out of any comfortable rhetorical delectation of the impressive facade, by the darker, grittier, morbid underbelly of Paris, whose uncontained flocks of the dispossessed embedded in him a new found anxiety and terror. Paris was the necessary rude awakening, the eradicator of superficiality and dandified sloth. Here one had to realise one's purpose, to work or go under; the simmering of the crowds constantly restated the danger of anonymity and separateness.

From the moment he arrived at the fag end of summer in 1902, Rilke was assaulted by a range of contrasting emotions the city aroused through its unrestrained action, an intoxication of impressions which are liberally recounted in Betz's essay and which drip-feed into the *Notebooks*. Betz focuses his book on the Rodin period, but opens with Rilke's first probings of the city and those preliminary five tentative weeks at 11 rue Toullier, where Rilke abruptly switched family and the communal atmosphere of the artists' colony in Worpswede for isolation in a dingy cramped student hotel near the Sorbonne. Here, in a kind of self-imposed claustrophobia, he would write long into the evening, by candlelight, since the fumes of the paraffin lamp nauseated him, drawn close to the rickety stove for warmth. The room in rue Toullier was like Paris itself, 'over-experienced' and worn out by the unceasing procession of occupants. Rilke felt the weight of the lives that had passed through it, imagining the string of tired heads that had, over time, worn a greasy patch on the back of the old armchair. Here he felt as never before a sense of feverish suffocation and complained of the ranks of windows opposite watching him like eyes, their 'inquisitive glances' somehow trained on him alone. (The windows as 'eyes' perhaps reflects his then reading of Belgian poet Georges Rodenbach's writings on Bruges.) Furthermore, he laments the high austere wall outside his window 'cutting off his breathing'. Right away the sense that the external is threatening his equilibrium and, as Betz says, 'forcing him to participate against his will', is emphatically established.

Some of the most intense early passages in the *Notebooks* are culled from this period 'lying five flights up' at 11 rue Toullier, where Rilke expounds his 'fears' with a new, pronounced morbidity. In these brief passages, fairly quivering with existential despair, one might plausibly suggest Rilke the modern poet is born. Mostly he wrote letters to Clara, daily round-ups of his impressions of an urban landscape peopled by a veritable *danse macabre* of the lonely and lost, traversing this 'strange, strange city' which seemed to be 'rushing headlong out of orbit like a planet, towards some terrible cataclysm'. The overriding atmosphere in all Rilke's communication is one of the overt presence of death, exemplified by the hospitals that he sees on his perambulations. 'I see now why they figure so often in Verlaine, Baudelaire and Mallarmé, you suddenly feel that in this city there are legions of the sick, armies of the dying, whole populations of the dead.' He describes stumbling upon these 'long hospitals, their gates standing open in a gesture of impatient and greedy compassion.' His hospital phobia climaxes with observations of the Hôtel-Dieu (See 'Notes on Places'), where he witnesses a patient being brought in, 'propped up in an open cab, like a broken marionette, tossed from side to side with every motion, with a horrible abscess on his long, grey dangling neck'. On another occasion he breaks off his journey to follow for hours a man with St Vitus' dance, as he hops uncannily along the boulevards to the gleeful interest of the café waiters and shopkeepers. Rilke selects such tragic figures, as he does later with a melancholy newspaper seller by the gates to the Luxembourg gardens, employing their monotonous struggle and the individual absurdity of their existence to provide an expressive ingredient for the precarious alchemy of his inwardness. But the intense indulgence of observing and absorbing such figures left Rilke wrung out and exhausted, 'as though the angst of another had fed upon me and drained me'.

4. Dusk in the Luxembourg Gardens

Although Clara had now joined him in Paris and he had moved from rue Toullier in October to more comfortable accommodation at 3 rue de l'Abbé de l'Epée, Rilke was still mortally afflicted by his experiences and it was from here that he felt compelled to write a letter to his most intimate confidante, Lou Andreas-Salomé, in which he poured out his anxieties at once, as if releasing a long-pent-up burden. Rilke describes his sense of ambulant isolation, of feeling like a 'pothole in which stale water has collected, which the hurrying carriages, instead of going round, drive straight through'. He talks of his fears 'expanding' and the 'excessively big city' being 'against me, standing in opposition to my life, like an examination I did not pass'. He talks of the people he encountered; the hordes that he feared would absorb his anonymous, perhaps superfluous body as one of their own. 'They wore the desolate, discoloured mimicry of the oversized cities and survived like tough beetles under the foot of each day that stepped on them, survived as though they still had something to wait for, twitching like pieces of a huge cut up fish that has begun to rot but is still alive. They survived living on nothing, on dust, on the grime and filth of their bodies, on what dogs let drop from their jaws...'

But Salomé rightly saw in this outpouring of angst and morbid terror not the catastrophe of breakdown, but an awakening, and the beginning of a new kind of literary achievement, as Rilke sought to write out of the pain he was experiencing, a cathartic process which would find its ultimate fulfillment in the verse of the *New Poems* and the prose of the *Notebooks*. Paris had unceremoniously torn Rilke out of his safe, somewhat fey nineteenth-century draped musings and thrown him headlong into the modern bear pit of a newfound expressivity. No wonder in letters he lauds the truthfulness of Baudelaire's torchbearing 'modernist' poem 'Une Charogne' (A Carcass).

This most necessary rite of passage, along with the encounter with Rodin, served to disengage Rilke from that reluctance to believe himself capable of working consistently enough to achieve anything of note. Paris and its vital energies swept him from the relative security and self regard of the purely artistic milieu in which he had hitherto moved, and sandblasted off any vestiges of literary self-indulgence still clinging to his person. Paris, with its monumental beauty but jealously guarded wicked edges, laced with that eternally seductive, bitterly romantic odour of possible defeat, serves as the necessary foil to his more reposeful aristocrat-sponsored residencies elsewhere. And although Rilke complains at the vitality of Paris being a false one in the sense that the constant frenzy of activity leads nowhere and only consumes itself, it proved to be his reaction to the unique self-devouring atmosphere of this city, not Berlin, Rome, Madrid, Hamburg, or Copenhagen, that counted in terms of his art.

At each consecutive address Rilke finds inspiration to write the most moving vignettes of his impressions without even leaving the confines of his room. None more so than those from 29 rue Cassette, in the memorable impression of a rain on vegetation beyond the window, or the appearance of the mysterious blind woman and her coin-collecting dog, which find a place in Betz's essay. Rilke's time with the Rodins at Meudon provides an insight into Rodin's troubled domestic life and one senses Rilke in his assiduously absorbing role, monitoring the daily rituals and feeling for Madame Rodin with perhaps a nod to himself, when he compares her relationship to the never tiring master as 'like holding a cup out under a waterfall'. The relationship between Rodin and Rilke was not without upset, as Betz illustrates, but despite the language barrier and Rodin's ignorance of Rilke's work, it is clear that respect even love was mutual and genuine. Each recognised greatness in the other, even though in Rilke's case the proof was still to come. What Rodin taught Rilke most fundamentally was that total sacrifice was the recipe for greatness. But this came with heavy losses: the security and joys to be expected from a more conventional lifestyle. He had to choose and memorably articulates this dilemma in a letter, which shows he had no illusions about the fate of his personal life. 'One or the other, happiness or art. The life of great men is a road bristling with thorns, for they are utterly dedicated to their art. Their own life is like an atrophied organ of which they have no further use…'

The simultaneous acquirement of lodgings at the Hôtel Biron was a physical endorsement of their close relationship. That it exists today as the Rodin Museum is due in small part to Rilke's urge to communicate the beauty of the environs to his friend, who immediately responded and joined him there.

By 1925, when he stayed at the Hôtel Foyot at 33 rue Tournon, Rilke's Paris time was drawing to a close. In failing health, he left a city that had provided a habitat, perhaps the only possible habitat, for that total sacrifice to art which was his legacy. Paris provided the premier cultural and historic architecture and necessary distillation of past atmospheres to enable this sacrifice. Baudelaire, Cézanne, Rodin, Valéry, Verhaeren… all these figures played their part in drawing Rilke closer to a regime of unremitting labour and the shaping of new experience within the confines of his poetic language at the deepest and most authentic level possible. Paris performed her roles equally convincingly, as both safe harbour and the threatening uncharted ocean beyond, as both siren and saviour, a lure to the infinite, immutable through the most violent storms or the dead calm.

– Will Stone, Suffolk, February 2012

5. Les Invalides from the gardens of the Hôtel Biron

6. Bouquinistes in winter, quai de la Mégisserie

Rilke in Paris

by Maurice Betz

Ah, The achievement of a small moon!
Days where around us all is clear, barely an outline in the luminous air and yet distinct. Even the nearest things have a distant tone, shrink back, show only from a distance, are not exposed; and all that draws on this expanse of distance – the river, the bridges, the long roads and the squares which expend themselves – hold that distance within them, and are painted there as if on silk. Who can say what a bright green motorcar on Pont Neuf might be, or this vivid red rushing forth, or even simply that poster, on the wall adjoining a cluster of pearl-grey buildings. All is simplified, restored to a few planes, sharp and clear, as a face in a portrait by Manet. Nothing is insignificant or without relevance. The *bouquinistes* on the *quais* open their boxes, and the yellow freshness or weariness of the books, the brown violet of the bindings, the more sovereign green of an album, all harmonise, count, take part in the whole and converge in consummate perfection…

From *The Notebooks of Malte Laurids Brigge* (1910)

The 'French Component' In Rilke's Work

The case of Rainer Maria Rilke is rather extraordinary: a Germanic poet in the deepest sense, who represents, in both its most intense and subtle form, a singular branch of German romanticism, at the point where he encounters the final ripening of the Slavic spiritual universe and discovers his own true identity through his relationship with a French city.

In Paris, this German poet discovered not only a temporary home and more or less enduring friendships, but also an inner inspiration, which guided him towards the secret configuration of his entire being. For some twelve years he returned almost year on year, both contented and disappointed to encounter there ever renewed ecstasies and anxieties, and a virtually eternal landscape. This city lent him the framework and themes of a work through which he felt able to express himself to the very limits of the inexpressible, to the threshold of reflecting on and accepting death with a calm heart, following *The Notebooks of Malte Laurids Brigge*, in which he was conscious of having marshalled the entire resolve of his existence. He gave himself so utterly to this work that after its completion he remained for many years stricken by sterility. For Rilke, Paris had been much more than Venice for Byron, or Toledo for Barrès: a revelation of the most profound possibilities, the 'dividing line of his inward waters' and the touchstone of his art. He declared on several occasions, with distinct emotion, what a debt he owed to this 'incomparable city which represents a world in my development and memory' and whose 'immense and generous hospitality' allowed him to bring into the light those feelings and thoughts which were tentatively seeking their form.

However important the 'French component' in Rilke's work, it did not manage to govern alone the deeper reaches of his being. This inveterate traveller criss-crossing the very soul and landscape of Europe, nourished himself on the nectar of all latitudes, without his fundamental architecture being altered. From one country to the next, he ploughed his unique furrow, scoring deep, sometimes losing himself in the most unfathomable subterranean labyrinths, but everywhere searching only that he might ultimately emerge into authentic existence.

In these scenic variations for the poet, one observes certain cycles. Some are of major significance: principally the Russian and French ones. The Danish and Spanish cycles allowed Rilke, on the one hand, access to the fantastic and the intimate acquaintanceship of ghosts, and, on the other, to that wide expanse of sky inhabited by Greco's supernatural angels, which haunt the *Elegies* and sustain the disembodied poetry. The Italian and Valaisan cycles frame these primary experiences: Florence and Venice are places of residence for the youthful poet who harmonises the first variegations of his impressionist palette, while towards the close of his life, the Valais afforded, following the deliverance which was the achievement of the *Duino Elegies*, the relaxation and relief enjoyed by a genial rustic poet.

In terms of foreign experiences, Rilke's discovery of Paris follows directly on from his encounter with the Slavic world, a religious and mystical phase which found expression in *The Book of Hours* written between 1899 and1903. France presented Rilke with a 'human landscape', which was mirrored at the same time in the works of her painters, in the lessons and example of her poets, and by that life so naturally expressive which is reflected in the faces of the Parisian street. 'It is ever more difficult for the writer to find in action the exterior equivalent to the soul's movements' he wrote with Ibsen in mind. The landscape of Paris offered one of those equivalents. For Rilke, that revelation would only deepen, until it spread throughout his entire *oeuvre*.

7. Le Pont des Arts

II
The Discovery of Paris

At the dawn of the century, a young man who had just published his first verses in Germany arrived at a modest hotel in the Latin Quarter. He had blue eyes, his curly hair was brush-like; his manner furtive and he bore the countenance of a dreamer. His high waistcoat and blouse buttoned to the neck lent him the appearance of a seminarian or young priest. A Russian priest more precisely, for his chin was graced with a faint blond beard and he sometimes assumed one of their characteristic smocks with deep folds.

After a journey of several months in Russia, during the course of which he paid a visit to Tolstoy in his residence at Yasnaya Polyana, Rainer Maria Rilke spent a period with a group of North German painters, at Worpswede, and in this Barbizon, set amidst the ponds and heaths of Lüneberg, had first heard pronounced the name of Rodin, by a young German woman who had for a time been the student of the great sculptor. This meeting was in many respects decisive, for Rilke began by marrying the young woman, after which, impatient to approach the master to whom he would shortly be pledging his profound admiration in person, Rilke abandoned this newly discovered home and departed for Paris, determined to meet Rodin and better study his work.

In the eyes of this young poet, whom an intimate experience or discovery relating to art bore so effortlessly over all practical and social realities, Rodin was the unique master, without rival. This lyric poet, still permeated by Slavic mysticism and fluidity, experienced a sense of revelation before the powerful blocks of stone on whose surface this man's sacred hand had the power to summon so many desires, sufferings and passions. And while waiting to be admitted into the court of the sculptor to whom he proposed to dedicate a work, Rilke wrote a series of moving letters to Rodin in which he compared the man to a God and his art to a daily miracle.

But what can Rodin have made of these demonstrations of earnest devotion? The master of Meudon was not insensitive to homages, even excessive ones, in which his virile ingénue assurance regained vigour and energy from the affronts of a turbulent career. Perhaps too, he detected in the enthusiasm of this young German writer, of whose work he would never have any knowledge, the sentiment of some exceptional quality. The fact remains that, after frequent invitations to Rilke to visit his workshops and share his table at Meudon, he would go so far as to offer him the hospitality of one of his chalets and confer on the young poet, like a favour of state, the responsibility of replying to his voluminous foreign correspondence.

This recognition came only after three years of active friendship, following Rilke's publications of the projected work. Rilke only remained Rodin's unpaid secretary for a few months. The master was a despot with the beard of a prophet; he had his moods, his caprices and rages. One of these storms dislodged, if it did not actually break, the friendship between the two men. In the meantime however, Rilke had discovered Paris and learnt French. He was drawn with contemplative obeisance to the forms of French life, to the Parisian landscape, to its writers and artists. To Maurice Martin du Gard, he later confided,

Every being in Paris bears a unique expression, a sign of their personality that they do not show, but that they do not seek to hide either. All the nuances of joy, of misery or solitude, only in the faces of the people of Paris do I find them, and the French vitality expresses itself in the multiplicity of these myriad apparitions; in the street I never cross a void; I go from one face to another, still bearing the memory of the authentic value and clarity of the first, and all is imbued with a consummate and delicate light…

The Louvre, Notre Dame, Chartres Cathedral, the spectacle of the Parisian street, supply him with the material for the new poems he is composing – strong contours, sculptural forms – all under Rodin's influence. At the Bibliothèque Nationale he reads one after the other, Froissart, Baudelaire, Flaubert, Francis Jammes… He is enamoured by the work of Paul Cézanne, makes the acquaintance of Eugène Carrière, Emile Verhaeren, André Gide, The Comtesse de Noailles. In the manner of several other German poets of the nineteenth century, Rilke is subject to the charms of the French language and its forms, and much later he even undertakes to incorporate a part of it into his *oeuvre*. He speaks with subtle perspicacity of the problems inherent to this language, the difficulties of syntax, the snares of logic, the riches and loopholes of its vocabulary. He translates into German the works of Maurice de Guérin, André Gide, Paul Valéry, a few poems of Louise Labé, Baudelaire, Verlaine, Mallarmé…and towards the end of his life, encouraged by the poet of *Charmes*, he even ventures to borrow this language, so long familiar to him, to expound in gracious and pastoral poems some of the enigmas of his heart and spirit.

The history of the exterior relationship Rilke enjoyed with France is however not the most crucial. These exchanges, however distant their consequences might be, were situated only at the surface of his life. The most crucial discoveries Rilke owed not so much to his French friendships, as to the fateful chance that led him into a solitary confrontation with the faces and atmospheres of an unknown city, the fundamental problems of life and the most painful mysteries of being.

On 28 August 1902, Rilke arrived at rue Toullier, already discomposed by the premonition of these forthcoming transformations. In a brief note, which, with a kind of coquetry he had prevailed to compose in French – 'In a French,' he would later write, 'for which somewhere there must be a purgatory…' – he announced his arrival to Clara Rilke.

There is no longer any doubt. I am in Paris, although the quarter where I am living is oppressive with silence. I am a solitary in waiting: what must happen? My room is on the third or fourth floor (I dare not count) and what makes me rather proud, is that there is a mantelpiece with a mirror, a clock and a pair of silver candlesticks…

Even five years later he would remember the strangeness of this first contact with the city and divulge to Clara, as they recalled a memorable birthday, his bewildered impressions: the Gare du Nord, the anxiety of those first moments, the long absinthe spoon which accompanied a glass of coffee, the post office on the Blvd St Michel which no longer exists, the leaves of the chestnut trees, that whole Paris at the close of summer, which he found right from the start 'filled with waiting, promises and necessity, even in its most elementary details'.

The comfort of the little hotel in the Latin Quarter was really quite primitive: in place of electric light, a smoky paraffin lamp. The back of the armchair displayed 'an indent in a shade of greasy grey that must conform to every head'; the stairwell was so dark that Rilke compares his laborious ascensions to Saint Michael's combat with the dragon. 'Ah! how terrible are those nights of the Latin Quarter in those little student hotels', he sighs.

Rilke only stayed at No 11 rue Toullier for five weeks. Towards the end of his stay, he complained that the twelve windows of the house opposite were trained on him like so many inquisitive glances, forcing him to participate, against his will, in too many strangers' existences. It was in this room however, that he began really to absorb Paris. When, two years later, he started to write *The Notebooks of Malte Laurids Brigge*, it was from this fleeting but unforgettable abode that the secrets of his imaginary hero would date:

To think that I cannot give up sleeping with the window open! The trams rumble clanging through my room. Automobiles roll over me. A door slams. From somewhere comes the clinking sound of a fallen pane. I hear the laughter of the larger shards, the faint chuckling of the splinters. Then, all of a sudden, a muffled sound, from the other side, from inside the house. Someone is coming up. They are getting near, are right outside my door, they pause, remain there a time, move on. Then, it's the street again. A young woman shrieks '*Ah, tais-toi, je ne veux plus!*' The tram rushes up all nervous jangling, then passes over, rushes on. Someone calls out. People run, they catch up with each other. A dog barks. What relief! A dog. Towards morning there is even a cockerel that crows, pleasure unbounded. Then quite suddenly, I am asleep.

Rilke bought candles for his silver candlesticks. He told Clara, 'In the evening they burned as if on an altar.' A soft light which he willingly contented himself with while waiting for morning. In spite of everything he began to feel at home. 'The people of the house,' he noted, 'are friendly and attentive (without having received any kind of tip).' Besides, he is a model tenant, returning home by eight o'clock, often earlier. A few visits to the museums, solitary walks, long evenings of work.

He writes these details to his wife one Sunday afternoon:

It's Sunday and it is raining. A slow rain, soft and autumnal. On the boulevards they are already heaping great piles of damp dead leaves; we have evidently missed our summer…

The initial impression of disorientation subsides:

The evenings now belong to me: I shall be contented with reading books, making notes. Meditation, repose, solitude: all those things for which I am most nostalgic.

In truth, it was first and foremost to make the acquaintance of Rodin that Rilke had come to Paris, and the master's invocation took on in his mind a virtue of exorcism against those obscure threats emanating from the unknown city.

All that relates to itself, will rise up around itself. Even perhaps Paris, this foreign city that to me is so truly foreign. I am in dread of all these hospitals everywhere. I now understand why they recur so often in Verlaine, Baudelaire, Mallarmé. In every street you encounter invalids who end up there on foot or in carriages. You see them appear at the windows of the Hôtel-Dieu in their strange attire, the pale and mournful uniform of the invalid. You suddenly sense that in this vast city there are legions of the sick, armies of the dying, whole populations of the dead.

Already we see seeping through, in these first letters one of the dominant themes of the *Notebooks*: the multiform face of death in Paris.

In no other city have I felt this and what's so strange is that this impression infects me here, in Paris, where (as Holitscher has written) the vital impulse appears stronger than anywhere else. Vital impulse, is that then life? No. Life is calm, immense, elemental. The craving to live is haste, pursuit. There is an impatience to possess life in its entirety, straight away. Paris is bloated with this desire and that's why it is so close to death. Oh foreign city, how foreign indeed you are!

These first weeks are however illuminated by the meeting with Rodin. In the master's sprawling workshops, in the peaceful garden at Meudon, the youthful poet glimpses the kind of bliss that might bestow art upon him. 'One must work, nothing but work,' Rodin teaches his young visitor. That is to say:

You should not dream of creating this or that, it is not enough to construct your own means of expression, and then declare everything. You must work. You must have patience. Look neither to right nor left. Lead your whole life in this cycle and look for nothing beyond this life.

'That's how Rodin does it,' repeats Rilke, like a refrain. He disengages from a too-centred existence, giving an impression of sovereign calm, of assurance against the blows of fate, which may perhaps be a kind of joy. But Rilke does not yet dare believe in this path to contentment, not least because he knows the equilibrium that it supposes and the sacrifices it demands. He remembers the malaise he experienced in the house of Tolstoy, the painful scenes which he endured with Rodin. These experiences imposed a conclusion on him: He must choose.

One or the other, happiness or art. The life of great men is a road bristling with thorns, for they are utterly dedicated to their art. Their own life is like an atrophied organ of which they have no further use…

In reality, Rilke had already made his choice. He knew that he 'would die of not being able to write'. If he had come to Paris, it was not only to gather together the elements for a study of Rodin, it was to ask this of himself: 'How exactly should one live?'

You replied to me: in working. And I understand perfectly. I sense that to work is to live without dying.

Rilke wrote to Rodin that 'yesterday, in the silence of your garden' he 'found himself'. He had understood that for the artist, work could be 'space, time, dream, window, eternity… And now the clamour of the immense city became more distant and all around my heart there was a profound silence where your words stood erect like statues.'

But what is the language of this city that remains when the tutelary shadow of Rodin and his great example recedes? Returning from Meudon, Rilke returns to the human stratum of Paris:

> Oh these oppressive summer evenings! Deprived of pure air, walled up in odours and stale breath. Evenings of anguish, as if trapped underground. Sometimes I lean my head against the gate of the Luxembourg just to breathe in a little space, calmness, moonlight, – but there too it's the same leaden air, still heavy with the perfume of the too many flowers they have crowded into the borders…This city is just too vast and overburdened with melancholy…

In the absence of the stimulating proximity of beings and objects emerging from Rodin's powerful hands, Rilke returned to books:

> Each day now I spend long hours in the Bibliothèque Nationale and I read much. In Paris books are most discreet; they speak to you slowly and in a low voice. This contrast brings benefits.

There were also art books lent to him by Rodin, monuments of gothic art, cathedrals of the twelfth and thirteenth centuries:

> It was truly a great art. The more one studies these things, the more one senses the value and exquisite quality of the accomplished work: for these cathedrals, these peaks and mountains of The Middle Ages would never have been achieved if they had to be born from pure inspiration. A long procession of days was needed and each lent a hand; so although not all could be behind the inspiration, at least they

were driving it forward. Everything has been said about these great churches. Victor Hugo penned some memorable pages on Notre Dame in Paris, and yet the action of these cathedrals continues to exert itself, uncannily alive, inviolate, mysterious, surpassing the power of words… I believe that in the middle of this metropolis they are like a forest or a sea; a fragment of nature in this city where even the gardens themselves are works of art. They are solitude and calm, sanctuary and rest in the ever-moving tracery of alleys. They are the future as much as the past, the rest runs on and drains away, rushes forth and falls… But they alone stand and wait. Notre Dame grows each day, each time you see it again it seems even larger. Nearly every evening, as night falls, I pass before it; at the hour when the Seine is like grey silk and when the lamplight falls upon it like cut jewels.

And here his gaze is cast upon another landscape dear to Rilke, the Luxembourg Gardens, at the hour when 'dusk falls over the purple flowers'.

Somewhere, a drum roll suddenly rises, swirls now here now there. A soldier in red strides the avenues. And from everywhere the people are leaving: joyful beings, laughing, exuberant, serious beings, doleful, silent and solitary, people of all kinds, today, yesterday and the days that went before. Some who have spent long hours on a distant bench, as if waiting – and the drum tolls in their head that they have nothing more to hope for – some who remained the whole day long on benches, snoozing, eating and reading the paper: all kinds of beings, of faces and hands – what hands! – now file out. It's like the last judgement. And behind those who are on their way, the garden grows. And Paris in contrast becomes narrower, clearer, more vocal and begins one of its insatiable nights, a night of spices, of life, of music and dresses.

The idea returns frequently in Rilke's letters that his stay in Paris is an apprenticeship:

> You can learn here, I think, but it requires a certain maturity, otherwise you see nothing. Firstly, because there are just too many things; next, because a thousand different voices are addressing you at once and from every side.

For the first time, on 17 October, in a letter to Arthur Holitscher, Rilke attempts to relive, with a little hindsight, his initial Parisian experiences.

> Can you sense that to me Paris is infinitely foreign and hostile? There are cities which are discontented and melancholy for being too vast. In vain do they spread, a little nostalgia makes them fold back on themselves, and their constant din fails to cover the interior voice which repeats to them without cease: a city is something against nature. Think of St Petersburg. But Paris is quite different. Paris is vain, embellished with mirrors, eternally overjoyed with itself, so content with its greatness and its smallness that it can no longer distinguish between them. Living beings follow the streets; you can't separate one from the other. In those first days, I encountered hospitals all over the place: behind the trees on all the squares stood these long monotonous buildings, with their great doors and their side gates set in high fortified walls. At the windows were affixed reproductions of the most serious ailments and the papers related in captivating fashion alarming crimes, playing with that kind of language which lends itself to everything and whose very terms are sensations in themselves. Yes, all was a game reflecting in other games. Ah! How I clung, with hand and foot, to those rare things which were different! To Rodin first, the great old man. To the things he had formed, to these silent stones, filled with restrained voices. I went to the Louvre,

stood before the Mona Lisa. I saw the Nike of Samothrace, which made me feel for the first time a breath of Greece, from an age when they still celebrated such victories.

It was there, the counterweight, without a doubt. But everywhere the atmosphere weighed heavy and as oppressively as the very first day.

I read a great deal at the Bibliothèque Nationale. Geffroy, Baudelaire, Flaubert, the Goncourts. I read, though the universal authority of this language discourages me. And apart from Rodin and Carrière, I still haven't seen and don't wish to see anybody, for the moment. I would like via some solitary path to arrive at work, to daily work, to the capacity to work. I wish to remain at least in the short term in Paris, because it is difficult. I believe that if one could manage to get down to work here, one might penetrate to a great distance and to a great depth. I first intend travelling to Breslau for my studies. But I could as easily begin them here. I follow courses at the Collège de France, I am going to read a lot… Something good will come of this. How long I will stay here, I don't know; in any case until early 1903…

Never have I felt so much nostalgia for Russia.

As much as he took full advantage of life in this city, there rose in him that anxiety which became the place where the images and feelings of *Malte Laurids Brigge* were gradually formed. 'Paris', he wrote to Otto Modersohn, who considered joining him,

is an oppressive and febrile city. The beauties that one encounters there, with all their radiant eternity, cannot heal the sufferings inflicted on us by the cruelty and turmoil of the streets, the contrived face of the gardens, of people and things. Paris imposes on my nervous sensibility inexpressible anxieties. It seems to have lost its way, rushing headlong out of orbit like a planet, towards some terrible cataclysm. This is what the cities of the Bible must have been like, behind which rose the rage of God to devour and overwhelm them…

Letters, over the months that followed, became ever more scarce. You might conclude that Rilke had sufficiently translated the first shock that Paris had given him. You might also suppose that he had sunk into his solitude and deliberately renounced letter writing. For:

What good is it, asked Malte, to say to someone that I have changed? If I change, I am not he who I once was, and if I am other than I was, then it is obvious that I have no further connections. And I can hardly write to strangers, to people who don't know me!

In the midst of this opaque and overly animated city, Rilke undertook to explore that obscure dimension from which he awaited the responses to so many questions. 'I possess an inner life that I was hitherto ignoring. From now on everything goes that way. I really don't know exactly what's happening.' During that winter of 1902 to 1903, he doubtless inscribed the feverish curve of those first pages of the journal, which later would take its place in the *Notebooks*. If it is true that

In spite of inventions and progress, in spite of culture, religion and knowledge of the universe, we remain only on the surface of life, if it is true that man has still 'seen nothing, neither recognised nor properly announced the living', then the first to discover this troubling void must surely do something about it.

This Brigge, this foreigner, this insignificant young man must sit down, and up on his fifth floor, must write, day and night. Yes, he must write, for that is how it will end.

And so it is presumed did Rilke, until, at winter's end, illness threatened.

'Perhaps,' he wrote to Ellen Key on 9 March 1903, 'it is Paris I can no longer bear, above all in this uncertain changing season, when the sun is so hot, the cool shade like a cave, and where all is so replete with disquietude.'

The Coast, the North, the South, all jostled for preference in his travel deliberations. Until one evening when the brisk trot of a carriage horse lead him across a barely discovered nocturnal Paris to the Gare de Lyon, from where a train would carry him to Tuscany.

8. The Luxembourg Gardens

.

III
The Genesis of The Notebooks of Malte Laurids Brigge

Nothing is more curious than following the evolution through which a work takes on its most complete form and in a sense emerges, before being actually written, from that ripening of inwardness, which had to precede its passage into the light. In 1902, *The Notebooks of Malte Laurids Brigge* were already sketched in Rilke's mind, and certain pages had probably already been drafted, as he was at pains to include rue Toullier as the start date of the *Notebooks*, which were in effect a transcription of his own private journal or of certain letters. However, it was only in February 1904, in Rome, that Rilke clearly conceived this work in its entirety, and imagined the principal figure that, distinct from himself, must be encouraged to see clearly into his own being.

Several of these 'imponderables' over his production and inner formation, whose influence Rilke had signalled, and putting aside those 'literary influences' through which historians too often seek to reduce an original work to the common denominator of its epoch, had converged to lend the *Notebooks* their definitive form, which is both of a private journal of a life, and a writer's dialogue with the faces that haunt him.

From his first contact with Paris, Rilke had borne this unsettling, grievous impression, which for a long time never left him and which would only be clarified much later. The overriding need to express these discoveries from the first moment sought some exit in the poet that he did not yet know how to open.

I know of no incantation; it is God who must pronounce it when the times are completed. I can only wait patiently. I can only bear with faith that deep source that lives on these long days sealed within me, heavy as a stone. But life is there, and it wants to use me for everything, my stone and me. So then, I am lost and I suffer…

It was Lou Andreas-Salomé, confidante elect, to whom Rilke spoke in greatest depth of his Parisian experiences – after a second and briefer stay in Paris, from May into June 1903. Certain noted faces, pitiable flotsam of the city, haunt him right up to Worpswede, in the mighty winds of the Lüneberg Heath:

> These beings, men and women, engaged in some meta-morphosis, passing perhaps from mental disorder to recovery, perhaps to insanity as well, all those with something infinitely subtle about their face: a love, a knowledge, a joy; a rather anxious and vacillating light which becomes clearer if only someone… showed they cared. But there is no one. No one who comes to their aid when they succumb to anxiety, to fear, to alarm. No one for those who begin to misunderstand what they are reading, for those who still live in the common herd, who walk a little askew, and then presume things are threatening them; for those who don't feel quite themselves in these cities and who are adrift there as if lost in a treach-erous forest, a forest without end; and all those for whom each day is a sufferance; all those who, in the tumult, do not hear their own will, all those who are submerged in anguish, – why is there no one in these great cities?

This call – discrete echo of the angst that Rilke himself never ceased to suffer – is reflected throughout his entire *oeuvre*; these passers-by, alone with their destiny, are the companions in solitude of Malte. The prose poem that Rilke cites in his letter to Lou Andreas-Salomé will find its way into *The Notebooks*, extended by a quotation from this chapter of *The Book of Job*, of which, he says, 'Word for word, all of it applies to me', and so will the letter formed from the recounting of a meeting with an epileptic, on boulevard Saint Michel, that Rilke reproduced almost word for word in his book.

So distance had not dissipated the phantoms of the city, and the memory of them, on the contrary, only tightened their embrace. There was now a pressing need to find expression for an adventure into the abyss that neither the romantic ballad of *The Cornet* nor the bright strokes of *The Book of Images*, nor the muffled accord of *The Book of Hours*, nor the rather affected naiveties of *The Stories of God*, had prepared the poet to evoke. So the idea of a Nordic hero emerged, a man both attracted and repulsed by the Parisian landscape, who would love this city, but must perish in having experienced too powerfully its oppressive presence, but who in so doing would concretise these confused ideas, assembling them around the central figure, the nebula of such impressions.

Two encounters crystallised the project. Of one we are informed by the confidences of Rilke himself. But the correspondence so far published does not permit us to establish a concrete date. Was it in Paris, or later in Sweden or Denmark, that Rilke heard the name of the young writer Sigbjørn Obstfelder, poet of an extreme sensibility, a subtle impressionist, who died aged only thirty-two, after having lived for a prolonged period in Paris, without having properly realised his full potential? Whatever the case, Rilke was struck by the fate of this young writer. He who, on leaving a performance of *The Wild Duck*, in Paris, and once again conscious of his Nordic affinities, had been attracted to this figure, a poet who he imagined melding with his own personal torments. When he decided to give a more coherent form to his Parisian notes, the idea came to link them in some way to this character and to surmount those interior obstacles of too personal a proximity, by resorting to the medium of a half-imaginary hero.

It was on 17 March 1904 that Rilke spoke for the first time, in a letter to Lou Andreas-Salomé, of his new book: 'A sort of sequel to *The Stories of God.*' On 15 April, in another letter to the same, he affirmed that he had begun a 'new work' on 8 February. Now, some time in January Rilke had read an autobiographical novel by the Countess Franziska Reventlow: *Ellen Olestjerne*, an account of which he rendered in the *Zukunft*. Rilke, who had met the Countess Reventlow on another occasion, was disappointed by the poor means of expression employed in this romantic biography about a young woman prey to poverty, illness and solitude. He wrote on 21 January 1904 to Lou Andreas-Salomé,

> This life, whose fundamental value comes precisely from what has been lived without being destroyed, perhaps loses too much of its necessity if it is recounted by the one who directed it and suffered it, without even becoming through all that an artist. One has the sudden impression that the human being it speaks of had not been the most important thing in that life and its conjunctures, as if, above it, life was born, and had not been properly understood…

How the poet's imagination surpassed the facility of these romantic approximations, to evoke the 'tiny suffering face of a strange young woman', and beyond this face the immense grey ocean, the low Danish coast behind the dunes, the castle of Nevershuus and its park… Such images welled up in the midst of a too opulent and fast moving springtime in Rome, and nourished in some way by the deception he had carried with him, for a book so impatiently awaited, rekindled his nostalgia for the Northern countries. And this was the second encounter that brought Rilke closer to his Danish model Malte Laurids Brigge.

But Rilke did not lend to the *Notebooks* straight away the form in which he finally presented it to his publisher. The Rilke Archive in Weimar conserves the manuscript of an embryonic version of the *Notebooks* (I) which begins with a conversation by

Malte with 'One of those rare Parisian friends', in front of a log fire. In a style of rather affected solemnity, which more recalls Rilke's youthful writings, than the dense and dark prose of the definitive version, the author describes the play of the flame, the distant face of Malte, his hands animated by the reflections of the fire.

But does this version pre-date or post-date the one Rilke undertook to write in 1904 in Rome? Perhaps one day this will be established. For my part, I return to what the poet confided in me many years later, on his last sojourn in Paris, in 1925, on the detours that led him, almost in spite of himself, to the definitive form.

The figure of Malte haunted me [he said], but I felt that I had an incomplete knowledge of him and in a certain sense only an exterior one. That is why, when I began this book, which at first presented itself to me as a sort of matching vase to *The Stories of God*, I had recourse to the dialogue form that I used to evoke Ewald and his friend. I was far from suspecting then what development this would have for the work in question and what imprint my Parisian experience would finally impose on it.

I was then in Rome. I lived for a few months in a little artist's studio that they had placed at my disposition in the Strohl-Fern Park. The lecture on Jacobsen, along with that so deceiving Italian springtime, with its excess of haste, had given me a nostalgia for the northern countries, where I still knew the good Ellen Key, to whom I had dedicated *The Stories of God*. I was writing a suite of dialogues between a young man and a young woman who confide their little secrets. It happened that the young man spoke for quite a long time to the young girl of a Danish poet that he had known, a certain Malte who had died very young, in Paris. The girl wanted to know more and the young man had the imprudence to divulge to her that his friend had left behind a journal, which he insisted he had no further knowledge of. But the girl protested that he show it to her.

For several days I managed under diverse pretexts to instil patience in her. But the girl's curiosity became only more active and she began to depict Malte in her own imagination. I realised that I could hide no longer. Interrupting my dialogue, I began to write the *The Notebooks of Malte Laurids Brigge*, without concern for the secondary characters who, in spite of myself, had brought me back to him.

9. The Luxembourg Gardens

IV
Paris Rediscovered

More than two years passed before Rilke returned to Paris. Sweden, Denmark, Germany welcomed him and successively detained him; his letters do not tell us if he again took up the work he had involuntarily begun in his Rome studio. Rilke renounced the study he had proposed to dedicate to Jacobsen, but he profited from his time in Sweden by perfecting his knowledge of Scandinavian languages and one might suppose that the Danish background to the *Notebooks* was established and intensified during the months spent at Borgeby Gard, at Furnbourg and Copenhagen.

It was at Treseburg, in the Harz, on 11 July 1905, that an affectionate letter reached him from Rodin, a letter that touched him so ardently that after having sent it to Clara Rilke, he asked his wife to send him back the original, 'to keep with me'.

My dear friend, I am writing to communicate to you all the friendship and admiration that I bear for man, the worker writer, who has already exerted so much influence everywhere through his labour and his talent. I needed to send you these tokens of friendship and these endorsements for your worker's soul…'

Rilke replied:

Thank you, most revered master… My soul opens to your words so that they might germinate in me. I think of you always. You know that… Bless you dear master, from all those to whom you give not only joy, but strength, solitude and the desire to live a more concentrated existence replete with labour. I love you with all my heart.

Thus restored at a distance, this friendship between the young poet and the great old man would draw Rilke back to Paris in mid-September.

'Paris,' he writes to Clara Rilke, on the very day of his arrival,

> is as sure of itself as ever. It is just the same, as gigantic and brimming with necessity in the detail as much as in its larger forms. Unbelievably real… I have become reacquainted with many things… I went to Jouven without even being recognised… Ah!
>
> In this city, three years are but a single day. I stayed sitting a long time in the Luxembourg. I went to the museum so full of people and statues. A light autumn sun shone from time to time upon the Seine and warmed a bridge. And all this, is Paris.

Rilke happily accepted Rodin's proposition of hospitality at Meudon. 'Life around the Master,' he wrote to Ellen Key, 'is like a river whose banks one does not see.' His days were divided between hours spent in the studio on rue de l'Université, walks at Versailles, Paris or Saint-Cloud, and the peaceful charm of the garden at Meudon, peopled by swans and statues. 'It's the very centre of the world,' he wrote, filled with admiration.

The relationship between Rilke and Rodin deserves a separate study. It is enough to recall here that Rilke was for the master, from September 1905 to May 1906, 'A sort of private secretary' until the day when an unfortunate incident – a moment of neglect by the poet which exposed him to excessive protestations – concluded in his being 'let go'.

This position, which enabled Rilke to be close to Rodin, has been interpreted in diverse ways. Rilke himself employed the term, in a letter to Karl von der Heydt: 'A private secretary of sorts'. But M. Angeloz reports that, according to the testimony of Jean Lurçat, Rilke would later protest against this label of secretary. In fact, it seems that the poet, in a bid to compensate for

Rodin's hospitality, had simply proposed to the master that he take on a portion of his correspondence during those times when he was with him at Meudon. But, as he later recalled to Rodin,

> It was as a friend that you invited me to come to your home. You yourself, you offered me your intimacy and I entered furtively, as you wished it, never making any other use of this unforgettable preference than to receive comfort to the depths of my heart, and that other, legitimate and indispensable, the authority to accomplish your business with your intention, before your own eyes.

The joy of living in the master's intimate circle had at first eased the burden of the tiresome work the poet had undertaken for him.

Rilke persuaded himself that in agreeing to relieve Rodin in this way he was acting as a true disciple. 'My pupils,' the sculptor had confided to him with a certain despondency, 'think they have to surpass me, to overtake me. They are all against me. Not one of them comes to my aid.' 'Rodin is truly alone as never before,' wrote Rilke to his wife.

But the two hours that Rilke proposed to dedicate daily to this correspondence had gradually overflowed to take up the entire day. Spring made him dream of Viareggio, especially when he was obliged to write for the fiftieth time that Monsieur et Madame Rodin were afflicted by 'a horrendous flu'. 'I must get back to a time for myself where I can be alone with my experience, where I can belong to it and transform it; already it weighs and troubles me, all that which in me is named metamorphosis,' he confided to Karl von der Heydt.

A shift in Rodin's mood, which from one day to the next gave Rilke his freedom, came unexpectedly to fulfil this secret wish. The master had dismissed the poet with a brusqueness perhaps to be found in his nature, but by which Rilke remained 'deeply wounded'. Nevertheless:

I understand you [replied Rilke]. I understand that the wise organism of your life must immediately reject anything which appears detrimental to maintaining its functions intact; as the eye rejects the object which hampers its view. I understand that and (do you remember?) how much I understood you so often in our joyful contemplations?

With a painful accent, but not without dignity, the poet bade farewell to the artist whose bewitchment, in spite of everything, he continued to suffer.

So there you are, great master, become invisible to me, as if by some ascension carried off to the heavens which are yours.

I will not see you any more – but, as for the apostles who remained lamenting and alone, life now begins anew for me, the life that will celebrate your lofty example and which will find in you its consolation, its honesty and its strength.

We were in agreement that in life there is an immanent justice, which fulfils itself slowly but without imperfection. It is in this justice that I place all my hope; it will one day correct the error that you sought to impose on that which has no more means nor right to reveal its heart to you.

On 12 May 1906 Rilke left Meudon and installed himself in a small hotel on rue Cassette, where one of his Worpswede friends Paula Becker had once stayed. Between two avenues of the Luxembourg, he managed to correct the proofs of a new edition of *The Cornet* and to review the manuscript of *The Book of Images*.

My room is small, but not too much so… not very well ventilated, but not stifling either, plenty of old objects, but those which do not bother you with their memories… Opposite, here, against the sky, the trees of the cloister; below, an old garden wall, covered alas with posters: a negro who shows his teeth, advertising shoe polish; to the side, Beethoven and Berlioz, Independent Artists in a washed out yellow; 'Bernot, end of season, generous discounts', in black and in blue on dark grey, the 'Palace Hotel' of Lucerne. But above there is an old ledge on the wall, in the form of a vault, scorched and bleached by the sun at its extreme edge, which always dries rapidly, a dark grey in its hollowed part and covered in places by greenery, busy with life and rustling. Further above, the chestnut trees, ancient, which extend their great hands, and higher still, always higher, a little to the left, the corner of a church nave, without a mast, embedded in the sky like a wreck in the ocean. And above, behind, and on all sides: Paris, of light and silk, faded once and for all time, as far as its skies and its waters, to the heart of its flowers, with the overpowering sun of its kings. Paris, in May, her white communicants who pass amidst the people, swathed in veils, like little stars, sure of their path and their hearts, for which they rise, set out and shine…

And the letter climaxes with an allusion to the hero of the *Notebooks*, which Rilke speaks of as a death that he himself would have known and that, doubtless, he will reencounter in his new found solitude: 'I think of Malte Laurids Brigge who loved all that as I did, if he had been permitted to survive his great distress.'

It was in this bright vernal Paris, less peopled with phantoms and hallucinations than the city of his early anxieties, that Rilke seized again little by little and staunched the wound in his heart caused by Rodin's unjust harshness. Days of labour, where the Bibliothèque Nationale took centre stage, days whose strict organisation Rilke defended from tiresome intrusion with an always courteous but inflexible firmness. And Malte Laurids Brigge, did he prove a companion during these long afternoons browsing old chronicles of French history?

'I am still a long way from Malte Laurids Brigge,' he wrote on 25 March to Clara Rilke. But even to regret being at such a distance, perhaps reveals that Malte was still very much in his thoughts.

A day of rain, observed from the window of rue Cassette and described with a virtuosity that makes one think of Jacobsen, places us right at the heart of the greenest pages, the most budding of the future *Notebooks*:

After several days of full sun, here comes the rain, and opposite me, against the wall, a gentle breeze returns the chestnut and acacia leaves, so that they all share in this dripping, experience it and all are shining from it. This is one of those days of rain that are not meant for the city. One must live beyond, on the outside, to see all this darkened green, all the meadows reflecting greyness, all the agitated numberless leaves in verdant luxuriance, for the lights have vanished (the clear, melting, dissolving lights), which are merely reflections: green, reflected by green, placed over green, shadowed with green, deepened green, and which somewhere are the innermost depths of green. And suddenly all these colours are drawn back from the perfume itself as if the sun, in vanishing had poured them into the flowers.

However, a few darker notes sometimes disturb the agreeable harmony Rilke now enjoys with Paris, leading to nostalgia for the countryside. For example, the incomprehensible laughter of the Parisian public before Ibsen's *The Wild Duck*, which the poet saw performed at the Théâtre Antoine:

The incredulous laughter of the Parisian public (public of the lower rung, it must be said), during the most sensitive, the most vulnerable, the most agonising passages, where merely the light touch of a finger brought pain. And right there: laughter. And once more I understood Malte Laurids Brigge, his Nordic essence, and that Paris had in effect destroyed him. How he had truly seen it, felt it and how much he had suffered by it!

Following a projected stay in Brittany, sketched out then simply abandoned, Rilke departed suddenly for Belgium, then Germany and Italy.

Once again, an absence of almost ten months, and a journey of the same length, which took Rilke from Bruges as far as Capri, via Berlin, Naples and Sorrento. But in June 1907, the poet was reinstated in his little room – well almost the same room, one floor closer to the rue Cassette. And this time he really seemed to have rediscovered, with renewed receptivity, the intuitions and anxieties of Malte, the fundamental tone of the *Notebooks*.

'Here once more, the Paris that devoured Malte Laurids,' he wrote to Clara a few days after his arrival, confiding in her the difficulty he was experiencing this time in acclimatising. 'The atmosphere of these furnished rooms is always loaded with disquietude and oppressive with disorientation…' And: 'That weight, the anxiety are everywhere here. Nothing has changed. It's always the same Paris.'

It is almost with surprise that in this foreign room he watches the blooming of a hortensia, which reminds him of the flowers in the courtyard of the Villa Discopoli. 'It never hesitates, it is so full of confidence, it already lives in this foreign room, for it only knows how to live.'

And the poet adds: 'But we, alas, we have so many other possibilities. We have far too many of them.'

Now occurs the encounter with that student – whom we will encounter again as Malte's neighbour, and whose nervous affliction ended up communicating itself so forcefully to Rilke that its manifestations seemed contagious to him, in spite of the wall that separated them. Rilke felt that this invasion of his being, this excessive responsiveness regarding other people, was a danger for his health and his mental equilibrium. 'This error would be excusable, if at least I was capable of drawing fully on it for my art,' he wrote to the Baron von Nordeck zur Rabenau.

But he feared not being properly prepared for the transposition of all too fresh experiences:

> For Paris, that I admire so much and to which I know I must submit as one submits to a training, is always in some sense new, and when you feel its grandeur, its near infinity, it annihilates you so violently and so completely that you must demurely recapture from the very beginning the impassioned attempt to live.

There followed a period of withdrawal, during which Rilke closed himself in with his spectres and those protagonists of the *Notebooks*: Death, Fear, Dream and Poetry. In October, announcing to his wife the recent visit of Mathilde Vollmöller, returned from Holland, he confides to her that this was the first living being he had seen 'for very, very long weeks'. For can one really count as human beings those 'ruined caryatids', the apparitions and voices of nameless passers-by, to whom the poet continues to devote a fervent attention? Marionettes, broken by life, who slowly drag themselves, like so many turtles, along the pavements of the city and make one think of strewn wreckage and those 'little old women' that so readily evoke Charles Baudelaire.

> Ashamed to exist, shrivelled shadows,
> fearful, bent low, you stick to the walls;
> and none greets you, strange fates!
> Debris of humanity for ripened eternity.

Then it's the step of a blind woman during the night, which prefigures another episode in the *Notebooks*:

That often does me good, to be faced with real night, the night of this little garden, for even a little garden may possess a vast night. (I was interrupted. I had recognised, down below, in the quiet rue Cassette, a light cadence uncannily repeated: it is an old woman who passes, who sings, as if she were cradling an infant. She is blind. A black poodle tugs on her left hand; on the right she holds a stick out in front. If a coin falls, the dog noses towards the place where it rolled, takes it and tosses it in the metal dish that his mistress holds out to receive it. While he searches about, she remains silent. Then, having launched to the heavens a final gratitude, she starts over as if she had never been interrupted, as if she had simply stopped listening for a moment. Now the street is once again in silence. From time to time, a footstep, from time to time, a carriage. Then, I recognise it, the stick of the blind woman against the pavement: She's back. It is time. For the ear this scene is akin to a view of the sky for the eyes; the same law enables the elements to appear, places them and orders them into constellations, all this, in spite of its distance, is replete with meaning and speaks to the heart of the solitary who understands and attaches himself to these voices converging on him, aboard infinite space…

So, during the fourth period of Rilke's residence in Paris, it seems that the fundamental images of that spiritual uprooting which was his Parisian experience had taken on their fullest meaning and found their definitive value. Though Rilke had during the last two years devoted a significant portion of his time to the *New Poems* (where are to be found in any case many of the themes familiar to the *Notebooks*, only driven towards a more formal expression), crucial fragments of the book were now transcribed. Letters, notes, journal pages – fragile testimonies, some of which have unfortunately been lost – formed the backbone of the *Notebooks* and were employed like sketches, studies of hands or torsos which the sculptor uses to prefigure a group work. Roughed out in 1902, tackled again in 1904 via the detour of a dialogue, which was in effect only a ruse of his interior demon, hounded by remissions between 1905 and 1908, it was only in 1909, in Paris and then in 1910, in Leipzig, that the poet would begin the definitive composition.

Formerly, in a letter of 17 October 1907, Rilke had admitted to his wife how much he owed to Baudelaire – the authority to integrate into his work the most horrifying experiences and to thus approach a totality of truth:

You will certainly remember a passage in *The Notebooks of Malte Laurids Brigge* which concerns Baudelaire and his poem 'Une Charogne'. I cannot help but think in writing of it, that without this poetry, the whole development of 'objective' language, such as we now think to see in the works of Cézanne, would never have even emerged: so this remorseless monument must be raised there, first. It was crucial that artistic vision was first overcome, to the point where could be perceived, in both the horrific and the sense of hostility, an existence as valuable as any other. Yes, the creator has no more right to turn away from any existence or to choose between them: if he refuses life in a certain object, he loses in one blow a state of grace, he succumbs utterly to sin. Flaubert, when he reports with scrupulous conscience the legend of Saint Julien l'Hospitalier, remains at the heart of the marvellous with a clear veracity because the artist in him participates in the decisions of the saint, approves them and acclaims them. He lies down with the lepers; he communicates all the heat from his body, right on through to the nights of love. Yes, an artist must go as far as this to ultimately achieve a new bliss…

At the same time (and for the first time), I understand the destiny of Malte Laurids. That test was without doubt beyond his strength, he could not withstand it in the dimension of the real, even though he was, in terms of abstract reality, con-vinced of its necessity, to the point of still instinctively seeking right up to the moment where it clung to him and never let him go. The book of Malte Laurids, if it is ever written, would be only an expression of this means of seeing, demonstrated on someone that it overwhelmed…

A day must come, one day, a time, for the calm and patience that will allow me to pursue the Notebooks of Malte Laurids Brigge; I know now many more things about him, or rather: I will know much more when he deems it necessary…

'The book of Malte Laurids, if it is ever written…' and 'A day must come…' These hypothetical or interrogative forms attest to the prudence with which Rilke sought to approach the authoritative assemblage of those manifold elements of his book.

10. Rue Cassette, 6th arrondissement. (No. 29 is on the right facing the wall.)

V
The Composition of The Notebooks of Malte Laurids Brigge

In creating poetry [Rilke wrote to Auguste Rodin], one is at all times aided and even borne by the rhythm of exterior things; for the lyrical cadence is that of nature: the waters, the wind, the night. But to give rhythm to prose one must go deep inside oneself and find the anonymous multiform rhythm of the blood. Prose must be built like a cathedral; there one really is without name, without ambition, without help: there upon the scaffolding with conscience alone.

And to think, that in this prose, I now know how to form men and women, children and old people. Above all I have evoked the women carefully crafting all those things that move around them, leaving a whiteness which is not only a void, but which, all around is tenderness and fullness, becomes vibrant and luminous, almost like one of your marbles…

This letter, dated 29 December 1908, comes at the time when Rilke, finally gathering together the elements of a book carried for so long in a state of virtual creation, pressed by his publisher, pressed more by the interior necessity to finish, undertook the actual composition, so to speak, of the *Notebooks*. Already in Rome, many years before, he had spoken of 'a tight prose without gaps' that this new book required. How different from *The Cornet* written in a single night, *The Stories of God* composed in the course of a week! This was a labour of prose the poet could not shrink back from. From the chaos of intuitions, of trial and error evolved a work of organisation, an arrangement following a precise melodic line, where the importance in comparing letters written in the immediate impression of an event and the definitive text of the *Notebooks* could be appreciated.

The story of this last stage in the elaboration of *The Notebooks of Malte Laurids Brigge* is principally reflected in the correspondence between Rilke and his publisher, M. Anton Kippenberg, director of the Insel Publishing House.

After having published *The Book of Hours* in 1905, this great publishing house gradually absorbed into its list Rilke's entire production, even those pre-dating this book. The foremost benefit from his alliance with Kippenberg, whom Rilke never failed to view as a friend and advisor, was that he could offer the poet both moral and material assistance.

In February 1907, Rilke alluded for the first time to 'my new prose work, which,' he added, 'only advances slowly.' In March 1908, in a letter dated from Capri, he expresses to Kippenberg the hope that he will 'be able one day to place it in your hands'. But the realisation of this work, he adds, depends – as much on his resumption of an essay he proposed on the work of Cézanne – on his return to Paris.

This return took place on 2 May 'in a peaceful corner where I am assured to secure a few months alone with a book I must finish'. And Rilke reiterates this confidence to Rodin saying that he 'reckons to remain in Paris for a long period'. The 'peaceful corner' was a studio on the rue Campagne-Première. Rilke preferred it even to the little house at Meudon that Rodin, in a gesture inspired by thoughts of reparation and forgetting past misunderstandings, placed once more at the poet's disposition.

The little house awaits me – alas! – for I, returning from Paris later than I had foreseen, after so much time involuntarily adrift, I must shut myself away there with my work: all alone. You can understand more than any other this disposition for solitude which takes shape in me now more powerfully than ever…

Immured in his home 'like the nut inside its fruit', Rilke only left for evening meals and met his wife Clara, who had re-joined him in Paris, just once a week. 'My book must be finished by the end of August and there is much left to be completed.'

Was he referring to *The Notebooks of Malte Laurids Brigge*? No, for he had already interrupted the prose work to devote himself to the second volume of *The New Poems*, whose manuscript he would forward to Kippenberg on 18 August, and which he had the pleasure to dedicate, further attesting to their definitive reconciliation, 'To my dear friend Auguste Rodin'. After this effort, the poet felt himself 'rather edgy and fatigued' and aspired to a change of air.

Clara Rilke had departed again at the start of the month, this time for the region of Hanover, leaving at her husband's disposition the large bright room that she had, in the guise of a studio, rented from the Hôtel Biron. In the absence of any more distant journey, Rilke felt he could find the necessary relaxation in this dream apartment whose bay windows gave onto a park of seven hectares. He moved in during the last days of August into the central large room on the ground floor where Clara Rilke had resided, then, seduced, rented for himself one of the rotundas on the first floor.

Rilke had seen Rodin again on several occasions through the months that preceded his arrival at the Hôtel Biron, and one of his first thoughts was to communicate the enchanting decor to his great friend, the poet's discovery of what would be the future Musée Rodin. 'You must see, dearest friend, wrote Rilke on 31 August, 'this beautiful building and the room I have resided in since this morning. Its three bays look out prodigiously across an abandoned garden, where from time to time one sees unsuspecting rabbits leap across trellises as if in an ancient tapestry.'

Here, finally, Rilke would find the necessary momentum to reengage with work, 'at my desk, in front of the open window'. Rodin, beguiled by the charm of the building did not delay in installing himself at the Hôtel Biron, and lent Rilke an oak table 'that will be the great fertile plain where I will arrange my manuscripts like villages', Rilke wrote to him in gratitude.

One of these manuscripts was doubtless the prose work undertaken in Rome, for the poet, since the end of December 1908, announced to Doctor Kippenberg 'rapid, solid and contented progress with *The Notebooks of Malte Laurids Brigge*'.

> I have entirely devoted the last months to this manuscript, for which I was prepared to go to extreme limits. I cannot tell how long this work will continue to occupy me (perhaps I will still be able to submit it within our prescribed term of August). But whatever happens, it is my resolve not to be deflected from this task, where so many disparate developments habitually encounter one another. It will be done.

On 2 January 1909, in the rare euphoria of creation, Rilke allowed his enthusiasm to burst forth.

> Isn't it just this way? You comprehend that a man who is only strong enough for one thing, sometimes crudely and clumsily worried, might be preoccupied with this single task; especially at the moment where he is owed joys and progress as strange as those which procured me my current work these last weeks. I could cite you so many beautiful testimonies. It seems to me sometimes that I will die when it is finally achieved: all weight and all lightness are concentrated so powerfully in these pages, everything there is so definitive and yet at the same time so limitless in natural metamorphosis, that I have the feeling of continuing in this book, distant and sure, beyond all danger of death. I do not have it in my heart, you see: the power to live come what may, and the right to live only for this work, closed in on it, supplied from outside by a little kiosk, like a prisoner for whom all things, even the least, take on their true value…

However, by the spring of 1909, three favourable months gave way to a period of uncertainty and fatigue.

You have enquired on the progress of Malte Laurids Brigge, but unfortunately I cannot reply in kind to all your good news. It is impossible for me to deliver the book for August. From one week to the next I hope to return to it, but the unfavourable constitution of my health, of which I think I spoke to you, has persisted; spring itself has not appreciably rescued me, to the extent that I am, after four months, well nigh unfit for all inner exertion. 'In this state of disheartened spirit, I do not dare predict when I will be able to re-apply myself to the interrupted prose work (of which barely half has been completed since January); perhaps it will not be until autumn. For it is possible that, as soon as my health is well disposed towards me, I will need to renew myself and to practise before nature and on my poems, to fortify myself and stretch out beneath the influence of the exterior world, the interior world from which I drew this book.

Moreover, this summer will be further disturbed by the fact that (due to a change of ownership) I am relieved of my apartment, meaning that in the midst of July I will be obliged to undergo a relocation, with all that this entails…

The evacuation of the Hôtel Biron was not as close as Rilke supposed, but this dread had contributed to a slow down in his output. On 20 October, he wrote to Kippenberg:

Of my prose work, half is completed; perhaps a little more. But the text is inscribed in little notebooks and on an old spread out manuscript; thus it is difficult to take it all in as a unity. Worse still, during last winter, working poorly due to my ailments and my feeble development, I allowed myself, against my normal habits, to negligent notation and confused certain parts; which made a copy of the whole absolutely necessary

This copy Rilke had undertaken himself, though he feared the exhaustion that this unattractive task would impose on him.

'What is to be done?'

Kippenberg's response carried a cheering suggestion. He offered Rilke the chance of a period of several weeks' repose in Leipzig on the occasion of his next visit. Thus he would be able with the lavish hospitality offered him by Frau Kippenberg, to dictate the text of *The Notebooks* to an experienced secretary, whom the publisher would put at the disposition of his guest. The impediment was therefore resolved to the satisfaction of Rilke and his Leipzig friends. In January and February 1910, Rilke was the guest of the Kippenbergs and in the tower room he was allocated, he could, thanks to 'a few richly filled days', put the final touches to this cherished book, whose manuscript he was loath to send in the post, even by registered mail.

In the following month, the proofs of the work joined him on his journeys to Rome, Duino and Venice. In this provisory and incomplete form *The Notebooks* already had a few readers, Clara Rilke amongst others.

> My wife began to read the *Malte Laurids Brigge* and spoke to me of it at greater length than of her health and her current life. I am happy to see her envisage Malte primarily as a personality, accepting it as such, and motivating her existence by being drawn back into the past.

Before sending back the proofs, Rilke leafed through them a last time.

> Yes, these *Notebooks* really form a book, as if they had never been anything else. What a feeling to see it like this, a genuine object amongst other objects!

Rilke had just won back his apartment on rue de Varenne when, on 9 June 1910, the postman delivered him the first copy of *The Notebooks of Malte Laurids Brigge*.

11. The Hôtel Biron, Musée Rodin

VI
The Book of a Sensibility

According to Ricarda Huch, historian of German romantics, the foremost characters in the life of a romantic poet are: absence of family, absence of homeland and absence of profession. Family, homeland, profession are all crucial links to the exterior world. Family, in Rilke's existence, barely counted: separated from his relatives by long-standing misinterpretations, he left his wife after the second year of marriage to obey the demands of his art more easily. (The prodigal son of *The Notebooks* flees his family for to be loved is too heavy a burden for him.) Born in Prague when Bohemia was still part of the Hapsburg Empire, he suffered the eventful trajectory of his native city, remaining a German poet by way of his language and his genius. Although around the age of thirty he had entertained the vague notion of studying medicine, he had never exercised a regular profession. His roaming existence across a dozen countries of Europe, and as far as Eypgt and Algeria, would on occasion have proved precarious if certain generous friends, like Werner Reinhart or the Princess Thurn und Taxis, had not loaned to this troubled traveller such remarkable places of refuge as the Castle at Duino or the tower at Muzot.

If Rilke's destiny was to be without family, homeland or profession, one could also say that in large part he himself had been the architect of this destiny. With rare exceptions, he had fled friendships and women with the same ardour that he had employed only a short time previously to indulge them. The fact that, towards the end of his life, he began to write in a foreign language is further testimony to that need for constant change and renewal. Attainment caused horror, in matters of love as much as in those of existence. His life was a perpetual flight before social and human realities, towards that abstraction which is solitude, towards that preservation of the absolute that is infinite desire, nostalgia eternally unsatisfied, and towards those superior states of consciousness which give access, in the midst of the most beautiful and sorrowful landscapes of life, to the contemplation of death.

A sensibility with antennae radically quivering, an over-demanding heart, vulnerable, tormented by a terrible thirst for the absolute. Rilke is this above all else. Realities only terrified him so much because all resonated in him too powerfully, because the least shock could wound him. Let us recall those painful and ironic pages of *The Notebooks* on the first deceptions of childhood, on those birthdays, for example, when one is always disappointed.

> The awkwardness and stupidity of adults are infinite! They find a means to enter with their second-rate parcels, destined for someone else. You run to their encounter and then you have to appear to circle around the bedroom for something to do, but without any clear aim... And it's the child who must warn of the faults of others, save up their shame and confirm in them the illusion that they are acquitting them-selves admirably. This, in any case, you achieve at will, even without specific gifts. A real talent was required when some-one made an effort and brought, brimming with impatience and jovial bonhomie, a pleasure – and already from a distance you could see that this pleasure was good for anyone but you, that it was a wholly foreign pleasure; you never even knew for whom it might best be suited, that's how foreign it was.

Such is the first contact of the sensitive being with life, and now one understands that the childhood preceding these experiences signifies for Rilke the reign of a perfection sadly all too ephem-eral. It is 'the time when you touch everything, when you truly receive everything, when you raise the objects that you hold by chance in your hands, with a power of imagination that nothing can deflect, to an intensity and fundamental colouring of desire which justifiably presides over you'. But why would he not prefer that 'wise non-comprehension of childhood', to the struggle and mistrust that foists itself on the human melee, when 'not understanding the embrace of solitude and that struggle and mistrust, are still ways of taking a full part in even those things that you seek to ignore'.

The poet, who exited this childhood and began life's adventure with such a raw sensibility, left himself open to experience the passions and emotions with singularly painful acuteness. In the play of the senses and the mind, the most infinitely minuscule, capillary movements entangled him, forging for him alone a peculiar interior life. The faintest impressions could enter into him, transform him, tie his senses and thoughts in knots to produce unexpected connections. Responding to a critic who had questioned him on the literary influences that he was thought to have undergone, Rilke listed Jacobsen, the great Russian writers, Rodin and Cézanne, then continued:

> But I sometimes ask if the imponderable in oneself has not exercised on my formation and production the most crucial influence: the encounter with a dog, the hours that I spent in Rome watching a rope maker, who, in carrying out his labours, repeated the most ancient gestures of the world, just like that potter in a little village on the banks of the Nile the sight of whom was for me a mysterious and inexplicable education. Or even when I was fortunate enough to cross the Provençal countryside in the company of a shepherd, or that an area as limitless as Venice seemed in some way so intimate… All this surely, is 'influence'? And perhaps it only remains for me to name the most important, to know that I could remain alone in so many countries, cities and landscapes, relieved of all hearing and all the obedience of my mind to the multitude of impressions, prepared to welcome them at the same time as freeing myself from them…

No, in these simple accomplishments that life accords to us, books could not have a decisive influence; many things whose weight settles on us through their medium, can be purely compensated by the encounter with a woman, by the change of season, or even by a slight fluctuation in the air pressure… for example when a morning suddenly hails a different afternoon, and through how many similar experiences we construct each day.

These emotions, sometimes dangerous, could equally become a strength for the poet, provided that he knew how to deepen them in solitude and thus live the most strictly personal of lives. For the error is to believe that we might somehow escape solitude and ourselves.

We are solitude. We can, it is true, grant ourselves change… But that is all. How much better it would be for us to understand that we are solitude. Yes, and to depart with this truth!

And what does solitude teach this supersensitive being who is aware of being 'an initiator in his own conditions of life'?

'I am learning to see,' says Malte Laurids Brigge. 'I don't know why, but all enters into me more deeply and nothing remains at the level where once it used to cease.' In penetrating this virtually incommunicable world, it seems to him that up to now no one had really understood nor even guessed at the most profound secrets of the individual. 'Is it possible,' he asks,

that all history of the universe has been misunderstood. Is it possible that we have still seen nothing, recognised nothing and said nothing about the living…? Is it possible that we can say: 'women', 'children', 'boys' and in spite of culture we don't suspect that these words, for so long now, have no more plural, that they are infinitely 'singular'. And to all these questions, one must reply: yes, it is possible.

Strange vision, which from then on he could apply to the universe! Limits blur between reality and dream, the present and memory. Things participate in life; witness the glances, which have brushed past, the hands that have leant on each other. Mirrors, have they not retained beneath their face the images reflected in them? Flowers, perhaps, understand life in their own way. Childhood, is it not wholly present in us, committed to images and sensibility, ready to spill out? In an atmosphere of dream or hallucination, the most fantastic correspondences establish themselves between minds, between things, sensations and images.

> The existence of the terrible in each particle of air, you breathe it with its transparency; and it condenses in you, hardens, takes on pointed and geometric forms between the organs… people would like to be able to forget much; their sleep softly files down these furrows in the brain, but dreams retrace the pattern.

And by who knows what poetic alchemy the real is suddenly evoked more powerfully, more surely than by the exertions of a more lucid intelligence:

> The road was empty. Its bored void drew back my step from under my feet and played with it like castanets from one side of the road to the other, as if with a clog.

Of this sensibility, which flows right through the work of Rilke, *The Notebooks of Malte Laurids Brigge* is in some sense a journal, immediate and routine translation. Reflections, landscapes, memories of childhood, coalesce and weave like the cloth of a tapestry. A young Dane traces these febrile lines, self-questioning, confiding his intimate discoveries, confessing the joys, anguishes and hopes that he experiences in his Parisian hotel room. The realities of the city oppose the strange apparitions of his dreams and hallucinated evocations of past events. All that troubles the life of this young hero behind whose features Rilke regards his own existence, drawn in some sense as confession, is delivered to us in a murky light, traversed by moments of mysterious phosphorescence, and in an apparent disorder, which already holds involuntary associations with the interior monologue.

Like Proust, Rilke broke up the framework of the novel and, without care for chronological order, he proceeded with successive plunges into time, space and his own sensibility. Here a unity of the human takes the place of rigorous artistic composition. Rilke believed that the un-coordinated nature of his notations would fare better than a rigid essay in maintaining the illusion of a complete life and somewhere he compares the thoughts of his heroes to scraps of paper from the dead that you come upon in a drawer.

A walk in Paris, a reading, an encounter, a window that opens and whose reflection projects a whole world of associated ideas, a visit to the hospital, a memory of childhood or travel, the discovery of a tapestry in a museum, a noise heard in a neighbouring room arousing the most bizarre thoughts, the sight of a house being demolished, a historic figure who takes on the relief or colour of symbol, a night of fever, the image of death, quasi-physical emotions, sketched or expunged sentiments, dazzling experiences, temptations, fugitive intuitions, all are pursued, abandoned, taken up again, orchestrated, analysed or formally realised.

This little book can be likened to life: in the complexity of the whole, it encounters the required things and those that are down to chance, parts which are wanted and others never achieved, some that succeed, others obstructed, from where a sort of infinity emerges which is not easy to capture in reasonable words wrote Goethe in 1829, speaking to Rochlitz of his *Wilhelm Meister*, but these words might equally apply to *The Notebooks of Malte Laurids Brigge*.

Through these evocations and resumptions of the real, Rilke explains, 'The young Malte seeks to grasp that life which ceaselessly withdraws into the invisible.' It is not in vain that he is the grandson of the old Count Brahe, who considers things of the past and those of the future as equally valid. The figures and symbols through which the poet exercises self-expression are not the idle games of an aesthete or variations of the virtuoso; they constitute 'the terms of his despair', are approximations to his wavering and tormented soul. But each of these characters is in themselves precise, wholly alive, and the meditations or apologues of the poet only serve to lend their existence a greater power.

This burrowing by Rilke deep inside himself left the poet worn out, as if wrung dry by over-extended effort. He had embedded so many painful hallucinations in his work, buried himself so deeply alongside his hero in the terror and neurosis that he himself felt, that whoever read the *Notebooks* 'against their current', the book might 'seem to suggest that life was impossible'. But precisely by expressing so purposefully his own interior persuasions, Rilke was to a certain extent saved. 'If this book,' he wrote,

contains bitter reproaches, it is not to life which they are addressed, on the contrary, It is the continual recognition of the following: through lack of strength, through distraction and hereditary blunders we lose practically all the innumerable riches which were destined for us on earth.

Instead of perpetually hesitating between action and renunciation, we fundamentally only 'have to be there, to exist, that's all, but in an immediate way, as if the earth is right there, according to the seasons'.

And when the *Notebooks* appear, Rilke envisages the future with newfound confidence. 'Now many things,' he writes to his friend Kippenberg, 'are, I think, going to reveal themselves in me; for these *Notebooks* provide a means of support... Now, finally, everything can really begin... poor Malte is a heart that embraces a whole octave, after him all songs become possible.'

12. Rilke's window at the Hôtel Biron

VII
Rilke's Presence

Here terminates the relationship of Rilke's Parisian sojourns with the story of *The Notebooks of Malte Laurids Brigge.*

After the brutal caesura of the war of 1914 to 1918, Rilke twice returned to Paris, in 1920 and in 1925. It was the universe of Malte that he sought to revive, and he stated in several letters how crucial it was in terms of his existence overall that this contact was re-established. 'It is still, – to a level that exceeds all expectation – my Paris, that of once before, I might say: the eternal,' he wrote on 19 November 1920 to the Princess Thurn und Taxis. And further to Mlle Elisabeth von Schmidt-Pauli:

> Yes, imagine, I saw it again, and from the first instant it seemed possible to live there with continuation assured. Ah! How my heart applied itself to the angry wounds of another time, corresponded perfectly everywhere, and was cured! What it meant to overcome that! It was only there that I knew how much I utterly depended on this reconnection with the world, the same place where... it became world for me, unity in one-self and transition towards myself.

And in a letter to his mother, Rilke even speaks of returning in more stable fashion to Paris, to 'transplant my life here, where the soil and air of my work exist'.

But this was an illusion that lasted only a few days. In 1925 Rilke encountered friendships, but also deceptions. It was a stay that proved a stimulus, but at the same time left him with the inevitable exhaustion of a long drawn out benefaction. A number of his key friends of the past were absent: Rodin was dead; Verhaeren was dead. The 'great friends who knew' had vanished behind the 'horrific wall of the war'. 'Their death,' lamented Rilke, in a letter to his wife in November 1917, 'becomes vague and unrecognisable; I sense only that they will not be there when the dread vapour dissipates, and that they will not be able to assist those who are obliged to set the world back on its feet...'

These absences Rilke strove to forget as he set off to rediscover the Paris of *Malte Laurids*, the Paris of another age, devoting long hours finalising the French translation of the *Notebooks*, which I was at that moment bringing to fruition. Old friendships had survived the war and new ones were born. Rilke saw André Gide again, in preparation for his journey to the Congo, André Gide who, fifteen years earlier, was the first to translate a few pages of the *Notebooks* into French. Rilke suffered somewhat from the scarcity of his meetings with Paul Valéry and from the too-evasive and nonchalant sympathy of the poet of *Charmes*. He met Léon-Paul Fargue, Alfred Fabre-Luce, Edmond Jaloux, Jules Supervielle, Jean-Luois Vaudoyer; he saw again the Comtesse de Noailles, deploring that these encounters often took place in a socialite atmosphere of commercial superficiality.

Rilke spoke in his *Auguste Rodin* of the misunderstandings that gather around the works of great artists. One might ask if the story of a number of his French friendships, if such an account was ever written, might constitute such mistakes. The ignorance of Rodin and Valéry towards Rilke's work necessarily limited their friendship, which was therefore reduced to a unilateral gift. André Gide, all intelligence and critical verve, renounced his projects to translate the *The Cornet* and the *Notebooks*. Valéry was perplexed by this 'maltreatment of intimacy' and with the silence and unbroken solitude in which his German translator indulged. Rilke himself kept a certain distance from the mind games and word play of Léon-Paul Fargue, and exhibited a retractile sensibility towards those socialite reunions, where the 'muddled and substandard crowd,' he wrote to a Miss Barney, 'threatened to become the symbol of my Parisian sojourn'.

Towards the end of August, Rilke fled, without bidding farewell, as if struck by a sudden illness, to plunge himself in 'fertile forgetting'. 'An exit sometimes has these holes in which one disappears,' he wrote to me a little later. It was Muzot and not Paris which would prove the cradle of his new work, *The Duino Elegies*.

I would have liked to quote here some of those admirable letters, spread over the long years, in which Rilke retraced or mitigated some line of the *Notebooks*, commenting on and developing the spiritual message contained in the book. But to do so would overburden the design of this fleet essay.

The Notebooks of Malte Laurids Brigge was reviewed in *La Nouvelle Revue Française* on 1 July 1911. The first critic in France to comment on them, Saint-Hubert, said 'These notes did not amount to a beautiful, well-constructed, well-made book. Furthermore they have something too raw about them, too abundant, too youthful, a barely mastered trembling; they are however exquisite and significant, heavy with the mystery of living works.'

Twenty years later it was still this quivering of life, this personal mystery, that French readers sought in the book. The moral atmosphere they breathed there determined the warm welcome the poet continued to receive in France, and that aura-like atmosphere in which his personality remains enveloped.

Robert Brasillach remembers one day, concerning Rilke, a subtle distinction made by Albert Thibaudet between the different sorts of radiance issuing from great poets. There is, said the author of *Les Heures de l'Acropole*, a 'position' with Victor Hugo, whereas with Lamartine or Baudelaire, there is a 'presence', meaning that the work of the first is a block sculpted across centuries, a colossus before which one stands rooted, while the work of the others has rather a fluidity, a familiarity, an ambience, a recourse and an assistance to the everyday.

In a not dissimilar way, one might say there is a 'presence' with Rilke. If this poet dwells beside us like a veritable shadow, if he offers a singular warmth and friendship, this doubtless emerges from the explicit nature of his work, in which, entirely intoxicated with itself, a soul is infinitely reflected, a soul which appears unique. But it is also because such an acute sensibility for the Parisian landscape is fused with the perspective of solitude, and because this poetry is richly interwoven with so many images and faces that seem familiar to us. In seeking to express in his own way the world we thought we knew, Rilke helps us to hear more clearly what already belongs to us and permits us access to the most sinuous and iridescent forms, to profound emotive states and to that strange melody of the interior life.

Alighting on this or that aspect of the *oeuvre*, one could say that Rilke was the poet of death, the poet of anguish, the poet of solitude and of the inner life, the poet of things, the poet of angels and the life of the soul… and there is clearly an element of truth in all these easily reached-for labels, but each of them proceeds with some innate restriction and each translates a preference where something arbitrary may enter.

The reason, it seems to me, that we experience so much difficulty enclosing this writer in a wide enough definition, is first the need for metamorphosis and flight from himself, which he never ceased to obey until the close of his life; and also because one must keep separate in Rilke the writer and the destiny.

His *oeuvre* is both that of a magician and that of a pure poet, and also the astonishing testimony of a life, a lesson in human experience. Although *The Notebooks of Malte Laurids Brigge* is a confession and a lyrical novel of sorts, a study in psychology and a treatise on the interior life, the work as a whole demands to be understood on a number of different levels. Rilke, who was an artist to the tips of his fingers, at the same time felt he was the bearer of a kind of message. If he had only expressed himself through metaphors and parables, in true poet style, he would have denied this instruction lay within him. Perhaps it is this that still contributes to his art and the strange fascination that he exercises over so many readers.

'If you read attentively *The Notebooks of Malte Laurids Brigge*,' wrote Edmond Jaloux, 'what strikes you most forcefully is that the refinement of form never diminishes at any moment the prodigious realities of life… It seems right, that to many readers of the *Notebooks*, this mysterious and moving treatment of the nature of life which is ever more absent from our literature, forms the backbone of Rainer Maria Rilke's meditations.'

In Rilke we observe a moving example of maturation through solitude and lucid contemplation of the loftiest problems of life, but equally an artist who expresses himself in a continual struggle to make explicit in poetic terms the fruit of that inner quest. These two images of Rilke cannot be separated; let us safeguard them equally and not permit one to overshadow or overlap the other.

13. Plaque honouring Rilke's discovery of and residence in the Hôtel Biron, 1908–1911

Notes on Places

The French Component in Rilke's Work

Maurice Barrès in Toledo

Maurice Barrès (1862–1923): French novelist, journalist and nationalist politician. Barrès visited Toledo in Spain and wrote the travel book *Greco ou le secret de Tolède* (Greco or the secret of Toledo) in 1911, in which he sought to interpret El Greco within his native landscape. In an essay on the Spanish painter, the writer John Cowper Powys penned an imaginative criticque of Barrès' Toledo book, castigating the Frenchman for his 'irrelevant watercolours of prancing moors, learned Jews and picturesque Visi-Goths,' and concludes: '*The Secret of Toledo* is a charming book, with illuminating passages, but it is too logical, too plausible, too full of the preciosity of dainty generalization, to reach the dark and arbitrary soul, either of Spain or of Spain's great painter.'

Very little of Barrès' work has found its way into English which is a shame, since he is a rather intoxicating and headstrong figure of fascinating contradictions.

The Discovery of Paris

Tolstoy at Yasnaya Polyana

During their Russian odyssey, in August 1900, Rilke, accompanied by Lou Andreas-Salomé, paid an impromptu visit to Leo Tolstoy at his home of Yasnaya Polyana. Unfortunately, despite having telegrammed in advance, they arrived during a family row, where the sound of weeping met them from adjoining rooms and the Countess seemed rankled by their arrival. Somewhat distraught, the pair were glad to escape into the park surrounding Tolstoy's modest house. There they walked with the great novelist, whose white beard, according to Rilke, 'fluttered in the breeze', whilst his face remained 'impassive, as if untouched by the storm'. Finally Rilke, seeking a possible master in Tolstoy, timidly confessed to the old man that he was a poet, upon which Tolstoy merely launched into a prolonged vitriolic tirade against art. Rilke and his companion then walked back to the train station through meadows of wild flowers on empty stomachs.

Worpswede

A village near Bremen in Northern Germany, in whose artist colony Rilke settled from 1900, following a brief initial stay in 1898. He was invited there by Heinrich Vogeler, a member of the colony whom Rilke had met in Florence during the period in which he studied Italian art. During his second, longer sojourn, Rilke truly entered the atmosphere of the colony and became intimate with Clara Westhoff, a sculptress and former pupil of Rodin whom Rilke later married, and Paula Becker, wife of Otto Modersohn, who as an artist is now known as Paula Modersohn-Becker. When she died following childbirth in

1907, Rilke was deeply affected and wrote the long poem *Requiem* in her memory. After marrying Clara, Rilke and his new wife set up home in Westerhede, a village near Worpswede, and remained there until his departure for Paris in the autumn of 1902.

Meudon

In September 1893 Auguste Rodin successfully negotiated a rent of 2,000 francs a year for a modest red-brick house, named the Villa des Brillants, in Meudon, a suburb south-west of Paris. In 1895 he bought the house outright. It was in poor shape and visitors were therefore rarely encouraged until after 1900. But what transformed the Meudon emplacement was the erection of the sculptor's pavilion, the new viewing gallery, which Rodin was eager to show off to friends. One of them described it thus:

> It harbours such luminous colours, and seems to dominate the valley of the Seine. From a distance you can see the elegant arcades of the loggia that make up the facades. From down in the valley, where the river follows its peaceful course… you look up and see this serene edifice, a temple of great art.

Rodin was most contented living amongst his creations, and Meudon became a constantly developing working area and home combined. Electricity was installed in 1904, but the house remained simple and spartan. Rodin's focus was on his sculpture pavilion and here he created a museum of antiquities, collecting Roman sculptures from his recent visits to Italy. Rilke arrived at Meudon in August 1902 and found Rodin 'kind and gentle' with a laugh which seemed to him 'embarrassed and at the same time joyful'. The simple and unpretentious lifestyle the now world-famous Rodin chose to adopt at Meudon was noticed also by the

Austrian writer Stefan Zweig when he visited in 1905. With the Belgian poet Emile Verhaeren also in mind, he observed that

> great men are nearly always the simplest in their way of living. In the home of this man, whose fame was universal, and whose work was as familiar to men of our generation as an old friend, we ate as simply as at a plain farmer's table, a good piece of meat, a few olives, plenty of fruit, and a *vin du pays*.

14. 11 rue Toullier, Rilke's first address in Paris

Rue Toullier

Rilke's first down-at-heel address in Paris, situated in the 5th arrondissement, close to the Panthéon, just off the rue Soufflot. Rilke was a stone's throw from the Luxembourg gardens and the Sorbonne, at the heart of the student district of Paris.

The Bibliothèque Nationale

The national library of France serves as the archive of all that is published in France, its prodigious collections dating from 1368. The old library building, which Rilke frequented, was built in 1868, and is situated on the rue de Richelieu just north of the Palais Royal and the Louvre. By the end of the nineteenth century it had become reputedly the largest repository of books in the world. Here Rilke would retire from the oppressive influence of the streets and occupy himself on an almost daily basis during his initial period in Paris, with the discovery and study of French literature and art.

The Hôtel-Dieu

The oldest hospital in Paris, the 'Hotel of God' is situated on the Isle de la Cité, near Notre Dame. Up to 1908, during the period when Rilke encountered the hospital, the Augustine sisters cared for the sick. They provided food and shelter to an army of invalids whose sufferings en route to its gates and behind its windows Rilke so memorably interprets. Because of its central location, the Hôtel-Dieu took in the emergency cases and still fulfills this role today, though with a much reduced number of beds. Such hospitals, with their incarcerated populations of spectral white-robed inmates, also chafed on the morbid sensitivity of a number of poets contemporaneous with

Rilke, such as Georg Trakl and Maurice Maeterlinck. For Rilke, who had claimed, 'In those first days, I encountered hospitals all over the place. Behind the trees on all the squares, stood these long monotonous buildings…' the Hôtel-Dieu was the main collection point for all those 'broken marionettes', the unnamed and unrecognized human flotsam and jetsam of the city whose individual expressive intensity by turns fascinated, appalled and exhausted him.

The Luxembourg Gardens

Always on his doorstep whatever his address, the Luxembourg gardens were Rilke's preferred oasis of calm and a crucial location for reflection and reading across all his Parisian residences. The Luxembourg is the lung, the central open space in Rilke's Paris, where the crowded tumultuous streets give way to uncluttered perspectives, quiet avenues, noble statuary and above all, light. The gardens were constructed on the order of Marie de Medicis, widow of Henry IV, in 1611 and were designed to echo her palace gardens in Florence. In some parts little changed from Rilke's day, they harbour around 100 statues, fountains and monuments. One of Rilke's favourite corners was the Medici Fountain, dating from 1630, now situated on the eastern side of the gardens, with its distinctive ivy topiary-like bordering the long rectangular pool. Though there is no bust of Rilke in the gardens he so treasured, a number of French poets he most admired are present, namely Verlaine and Baudelaire, along with other notables such as Beethoven and George Sand.

The Genesis of The Notebooks of Malte Laurids Brigge

The Castle of Nevershuus

The mysterious location for part of Countess Reventlow's auto-biographical novel, Schloss Nevershuus and its park, occupied a lonely stretch of the Danish coast. According to Betz, the melancholy atmosphere of this romantic castle exacerbated a nostalgic longing for northern latitudes in Rilke, who was already a perceptive interpreter of the sensorial tales of Jens Peter Jacobsen.

The Strohl-Fern Park, Rome

Rilke occupied a simple cottage here in the gardens of the Villa Strohl-Fern, near the Villa Borghese in Rome, throughout the autumn of 1903. In one of his 'Letters to a Young Poet', Rilke states: 'in a few weeks I will move into a quiet, simple room, an old summerhouse, which lies lost deep in a large park, hidden from the city, its noises and incidents. There I will live all winter and enjoy the great silence, from which I expect the gift of happy, work-filled hours.' Alfred Wilhelm Strohl-Fern (1847–1927), the architect of the villa and gardens, encouraged artists to stay amidst mature cedars, cypresses, elders and pines and a wealth of Roman statues, thereby creating a colony of sorts, which continued into the early part of the twentieth century.

Paris Rediscovered

Borgeby Gard

Summer residence in Sweden, on the idyllic estate of Hanna Larsson, who offered the poet sanctuary in the summer of 1904, followed his stay in the garden cottage in Rome, where his attempts to continue *The Notebooks* had dried up. From here on 12 August, Rilke addressed an eighth letter to Franz Kappus, the young would be poet who had sought his advice. (*Letters to a Young Poet*)

'If only it were possible for us to see farther than our knowledge reaches, and even a little beyond the outworks of our presentiment, perhaps we would bear our sadnesses with greater trust than we have in our joys. For they are the moments when something new has entered us, something unknown; our feelings grow mute in shy embarrassment, everything in us withdraws, a silence arises, and the new experience, which no one knows, stands in the midst of it all and says nothing.'

Treseburg

A picturesquely situated medieval town in the Harz region of Germany, with a castle perched above a bend in the river. Here Rilke stayed overnight in July 1905, according to Rilke biographer Ralph Freedman, to deliver a basket of strawberries and apples from Lou Salomé's garden to a friend. It was here, Betz suggests, Rilke received the crucial letter from Rodin, which helped to staunch the wound of their separation.

Viareggio

A popular historic coastal town in northern Tuscany with an unusually high density of handsome art nouveau buildings. Famous for its carnivals and, perhaps, for Rilke.

15. Rue Cassette, 6th arrondissement, Paris

Rue Cassette

Rilke moved into a modest room at 29 rue Cassette in the 6th arrondissement, near Place Saint Sulpice, on 12 May 1906, after taking leave of Rodin's hospitality at Meudon. In new-found solitude, he wrote down some of the memorable impressions garnered from his fortunate location in a quiet lane near the Luxembourg, opposite a church whose nave was 'embedded in the sky like a wreck in the ocean', separated from him by a wall and mature chestnut trees, which 'extend their great hands', presumably in welcome. To visit rue Cassette today is to find a road in essence little changed. The church is evident, as is the courtyard, which Rilke may have described as a 'cloister'. Even mature trees are in evidence and the wall now devoid of the posters advertising shows and shoe polish which Rilke describes. Rilke left rue Cassette to travel restlessly in Italy, Belgium and Germany, but returned to the same address, albeit a different room, in the summer of 1907. As Betz states, it was at this point, during Rilke's fourth period of residence in Paris, that 'the fundamental images of that spiritual uprooting which was his Parisian experience, had taken on their fullest meaning and found their definitive value'.

Villa Discopoli

Still afflicted by the fallout from his rift with Rodin and exhausted by family demands in Germany, Rilke sought an escape at the start of the winter of 1906. True to form, his ability to gain the confidence of aristocratic women with implausibly long names paid off again. Rilke received the patronage of one Baroness Nordeck zur Rabenau, who offered him the Villa Discopoli on the island of Capri. The 'rose house' has since become famous as Rilke's idyllic Capri residence. He arrived on his thirtieth birthday on 4 December 1906 and stayed until 20 May 1907, returning in the spring of 1908 for a few months. However, content as he was in the 'rose house', Rilke appeared unimpressed with the commercial aspect of Capri and naturally recoiled from the behavior of German tourists who drank themselves senseless in a beer hall off the *piazzetta*. In the spring of 1907, His thoughts were turning once more to Paris and the restoration of that hard-won solitude he had reluctantly interrupted.

The Composition of the Notebooks of Malte Laurids Brigge

Rue Campagne-Première

In May 1908, Rilke found a new 'peaceful corner' in Paris where he might resume his work. This studio at 17 rue Campagne-Première, where Paula Becker had once stayed, was located a little further south than his previous addresses, in the area of Montparnasse, a zone which would later become the enclave of a new generation of international writers and artists. Here Rilke live in enforced isolation, cherishing his newfound solitude and feeling creatively upbeat and perfectly snug 'like the nut inside its fruit'. Here he completed the *New Poems* and presumably intermittently re-acquainted himself with the ever ongoing *Notebooks*.

The Hôtel Biron

It was Rilke's wife Clara who led the poet inadvertently to the majestic Hôtel Biron, which would be the future Musée Rodin, at 77 rue de Varenne, in the 7th arrondissement. Rilke, after dispatching his manuscript of the *New Poems*, felt drained and had expressed the need for 'a change of air'. He decided to occupy Clara's studio space in the old mansion while she returned to Hanover. However, he was so seduced by the venerable old building and its romantic overgrown gardens that he soon found his own rooms, and through his emphatic endorsement of the aesthetics of the residence in turn drew Rodin, who then also moved in. The house had been subdivided into lodgings around 1905, but only a few years later plans were drawn up to demolish the building and put up a block of flats. Rodin's presence thankfully subverted such a catastrophe. He rented several rooms on the ground floor for his sculptures, these rooms gradually turning into his studio proper. Here, at the height of his fame, he entertained friends and admirers from around the world. Fittingly, the building has housed the Musée Rodin since 1919.

The Book of a Sensibility

Duino

The location that gave its name to Rilke's most famous collection of poems, *The Duino Elegies*. 'Who, if I cried out, would hear me amongst the angelic orders?' must surely have more alternative versions in English than any other line of modern poetry in existence. Rilke had visited the Princess Marie Thurn und Taxis at the castle of Duino near Trieste in January 1912. He was feeling unsettled and melancholy, so he took a stroll along the cliffs high above the sea to get some air. The voice that Rilke apparently heard coming in on the wind as he walked by the cliffs, dictated the above quote, presumably in fluent German. The initial Elegies were formed at this visit in what was said to be a kind of trance, but the remainder would have to wait until the protracted trauma of the First World War and Rilke's mental vicissitudes could be cogently harnessed. They were finally completed at another quite different castle in another country, a decade later.

Muzot

The little 'chateau' of Muzot served as Rilke's residence for the last five years of his life. Situated high on the side of the valley overlooking the upper Rhône just outside Sierre, in the Valais region of Switzerland, it was the refuge Rilke had been looking for where he might finally complete the *Elegies*. Muzot was to be the chosen haven for uninterrupted work, amidst a rural landscape that was not so dramatic as to foist itself on the poet, but would genially accompany him in his labours. Thanks to the patronage of one Werner Reinhart, who bought the house and installed Rilke in it rent-free, the poet, in a veritable storm of creativity, not only completed the *Elegies*, but wrote the *Sonnets to Orpheus*, as well as some four hundred poems in French, many of which were dedicated to the region which had inspired his last years. Rilke died of suspected leukaemia at Muzot on 29 December 1926 and was buried in the churchyard of the nearby village of Raron. Typically he had chosen his final resting place with great care, a solitary position, dramatic yet not inhospitable, high on a rock promontory above the spectacular Rhone valley. His epitaph famously reads: 'Rose, oh pure contradiction, to be no-one's sleep under so many lids.'

Notes on the Melody of Things

by Rainer Maria Rilke

Introduction

Notes on the Melody of Things is taken from the fifth volume of Rilke's *Collected Works*, published by Insel (1965). It dates from the year 1898, when Rilke was just twenty-three years old. Few people are aware of its existence, and English translations are noticeably rare. I discovered the *Notes* myself through a German/French bilingual edition, published by Allia, Paris, in 2008, which I happened to review for the *Times Literary Supplement*. This little book was a popular choice on Allia's list and, priced at a mere 3 euros, could hardly be passed by. Some of the information from my introduction here was sourced from the Allia book, specifically a 'translator's note' by Bernard Pautrat.

The year before *Notes* was written, Rilke had been following courses at the University of Munich in Germany and had there met the enigmatic Lou Andreas-Salomé for the first time. This deeply attractive, independent, formidably intellectual, well-travelled woman had relationships with a number of leading intellectual figures of the age, such as Wagner and Freud, but was most ardently pursued by Nietzsche, whose volley of marriage proposals only glanced off the armour of her strictly maintained independence, a bitter disappointment which could only hasten the troubled philosopher's descent into self-loathing and mental chaos.

When Rilke met Salomé in Munich she was fifteen years his senior. He quickly fell in love with her and they lived in close liaison, travelling widely, even with Salomé's then husband, sharing their impressions and thoughts on mutually sustaining subjects. Salomé taught the young poet Russian, advised him to change his name to the more commanding 'Rainer' from the fey-sounding 'René', and became his chief advisor and confidante. It was she who began introducing him to intellectually minded members of the European aristocracy, initiating a system of patronage which was to remain absolutely crucial throughout Rilke's working life. And, most tellingly, she talked of Nietzsche and their platonic yet intensely cerebral relationship, drawing Rilke closer to the personality of the most essential thinker of the modern age and his writings.

In the spring of 1898 Rilke visited Italy to study Renaissance painting in Florence. In encountering the Italian masters, Rilke embarked on the first of a series of self-educating periods of artistic observation, which would continue later in Paris with the overwhelming lesson of Cézanne in 1907. But in 1898, he was only beginning his journey towards that distinctive poetry of inwardness that would make his name in the forthcoming century. *Notes* then appears to exhibit a double formation in a concentrated observation of the work of the Italian Primitive painters and the philosophy of Nietzsche, namely from the period of *The Birth of Tragedy*, published in 1872 when Nietzsche was twenty-eight. Elements of the framework of the *Notes* are to be found in the Greek model behind *The Birth of Tragedy*, such as the stage, the actors and the chorus. Other elements are taken from his reflection on Italian paintings viewed in the galleries of Florence, the foreground, the background and the isolated figures represented within a landscape. In this early work, *The Birth of Tragedy*, taking Greek culture and the perceived failure of a Socratic ideal as a template for the modern age, Nietzsche sought to sweep away the debris of a culture made decrepit by 2,000 years of Christianity, and reinstate a Dionysian one with the unrestrained and deliriously 'unscientific' music of Wagner as its figurehead. In the Dionysian culture Nietzsche glorified, the primordial unity of the world is achieved through the individual who only commits to the wider community by immersing himself in life in the 'here and now' fully, and by eschewing that vague appearance of existence which the Apollonian culture champions. To connect with this individual essence is to find new hope in a fully lived earthly existence, beyond the precarious promise of an afterlife. Such thoughts naturally appealed to Rilke, who abhorred the dogma of religion and did not care much for what he augured in the orthodox entrails of Christianity. In *Notes*, the constant ebb and flow between background and the foreground, solitude and community, choir and 'the melody of things', all implicitly echo Nietzschean preoccupations with the Apollonian and the Dionysian. And, like Nietzsche, Rilke is suggesting a reform of all values, a revolution of the scene, which will constitute an overthrowing of the current culture still fettered to outmoded thought and thus the construction of a whole new way of being. Rilke's urge to have done with the petrifying properties of realism and harness a new way of seeing is also symptomatic of his age and is copiously reflected in the works of dramatist writers of the period, such as Maurice Maeterlinck, Konstantin Stanislavski and Max Reinhardt. What's more, the symbolist period in art was all about suggestion, rather than slavishly de-picting reality, looking beyond the obvious to hidden identities within objects and landscapes, which could only be accessed by patient contemplation and a willingness to transmogrify plastic elements into a necessarily elusive theatre of the senses. This preoccupation is also present in the *Notes*.

But to reduce *Notes* to a simple manifesto for Nietzschean revolt or a radical text for the new theatre would be grossly over-simplistic. For it is a significant movement towards the poetry, which was as far as Rilke was concerned, only to begin properly a year later in 1899, with *The Book of Hours. Notes* is at once mysterious and enigmatic, tantalising and sometimes infuriating in the way it falls back like a wave from the sea wall of absolute clarity. It leads the reader into a labyrinth veiled with the most beautiful and artful webs that must catch on you as you pass. The reader should therefore harvest sublime moments such as: 'You must extract the rhythm of the waves' sound from the roaring tumult of the sea and from the tangled net of everyday conversation, somehow draw the one living line that bears the rest...' or acknowledge the typically Rilkean aphorism of 'Even when the root is ignorant of the fruits, it nourishes them nevertheless.' It would be true to say that these

Notes, miniature prose poems in a sense themselves, announce the great poetry to come. The particular attention paid to the complex relationship between the close at hand and the wider unknown immensity beyond, will always remain a recurring element of Rilke's poetry. Solitude, the giving productive solitude that outruns loneliness for a time, will always constitute its main artery and, as Rilke reminds us from the lower rung of his maturity, 'The more solitary a person is, the more solemn, moving and powerful their community.'

Notes on the Melody of Things

I

We are right at the beginning, you see.
As if before everything. With
a thousand and one dreams behind us and
without act.

II

I can think of no knowledge more sacred
than this:
That you must become one who begins.
One who writes the first word behind
a century-long
dash.

III

It occurs to me: with this observation:
that we still paint figures against a
gold background, like the early Primitives.
Before the indeterminate they stand.
Sometimes of gold, sometimes of grey.
Sometimes in the light and often with,
behind them, an inscrutable darkness.

IV

That is understood. To know men
one must isolate them. But after a long
experience, it seems right to put back
such isolated reflections into a relationship,
with each other and with more ripened
gaze accompany their broad gestures.

V

Compare just once the gold background of the
Trecento, with the numerous later compositions
of the old Italian masters, where the figures assemble
for a *Santa Conversazione* before a radiant landscape
in the light air of Umbria. The gold background
isolates each figure. The landscape shines behind
them like a common soul, from which they draw
their smile and their love.

VI

Then think on life itself. Remember that men
have many inflated gestures and unimaginably
grandiose words. If they were, if only for a time,
as calm and as deep as the beautiful saints of Marco
Basaiti, then behind them too you would find
the landscape they have in common.

VII

And there are moments too where
a man before you stands apart, clear and calm
before his splendour. These are rare festivals
that you will never forget. From that point on
you love this man. That is to say, you trace
with your own tender hands, the contours
of his personality as you knew it in this hour.

VIII

Art does the same. It is, yes, the most ample,
the most presumptuous love. It is God's love. It
cannot stop at the individual who is only the door
to life. It must break through. It must never tire.
To fulfil itself, it must labour where all – are a *one*.
And when it gives to this *one*, then for all comes
a richness without limit.

IX

How far art is from this can be seen
on the stage, where it says or means to say
how life is, not the individual in his ideal repose
but the movement and interaction of the many.
So the truth is, it simply places people
side by side, as in the Trecento, and leaves them
to forge closer relationships before the grey or
gold of the background.

X

And that is what happens. They try to reach
each other with words, with gestures. They almost
dislocate their arms, for their gestures are too short.
They make interminable efforts to launch syllables,
but they are frankly bad players of the ball, who don't
know how to catch. So time passes in stooping and
seeking – just as in life.

XI

And art has done nothing other than shown us
the confusion in which we reside most of the time.
It has worried us, instead of making us quiet and
calm. It has proved that each lives on their island;
only the islands are not distant enough that we might
live peacefully and in solitude. One can disturb another
or terrify them, or pursue them with spears – only
no-one cannot help no-one.

XII

From island to island there is only one possibility:
dangerous leaps, where one risks more than one's legs.
This means an eternal leaping back and forth,
with accidents and absurdities; for if it happens that
two people leap towards one another at the same moment,
they meet each other only in mid-air
and following this taxing exchange, they find themselves
one from the other, as far apart as before.

XIII

This is not at all strange; for in reality the bridges
that lead one to the other, over which you
travel with beautiful solemn step, are not *in* us,
but behind us, precisely as in the landscapes of
Fra Bartolomeo or Leonardo. It is a fact that life
really does reach a fine point in the individual.
But from summit to summit the path runs through
ever broadening valleys.

XIV

When two or three people are assembled,
this does not mean they are properly together.
They are like marionettes whose strings are
in different hands. Only when one hand guides
them all do they form a community which compels
them to bow low or crash into each other.
And the strength of the human, that too is there
in the one sovereign hand that holds the strings.

XV

Now they find themselves in the common hour, in the
common storm, in the one room where they find each
other. Not until a background is raised behind them do
they begin to consort with one another. For they must
invoke the *one* homeland. They must at the same time
show each other their accreditations, that they carry
with them and which hold the word and seal of the
same Prince.

XVI

Whether it be the singing of the lamp or the voice
of the storm, whether it be the breath of evening,
or the groan of the ocean that envelops you – always
behind you an expanse of melody keeps watch, woven
of a thousand voices, where only here and there
is there room for your solo. To know 'at what moment
you must make your entrance', that is the secret of
your solitude: just as the art of genuine fellowship is
to allow the lofty words to fall into the common melody.

XVII

If the saints of Marco Basaiti had something to confide
to each other beyond their sacred nearness, one to the
other, they would not reach out their thin, gentle hands to the
foreground of the painting they inhabit. They would withdraw
    to the
background, become quite small, and, deep in the listening
countryside, come towards each other over tiny bridges.

XVIII

We in front are just the same, sanctifying yearnings.
Our fulfilment takes place in the luminous backgrounds.
Only there is momentum and will. Only there play out
    histories
in which we are merely the dark headlines. Only there are our
accords, our leave-takings, our consolation and our grief.
It is there we *are*, while here in the foreground we
come and go.

XIX

Recall the people you found gathered together who had barely
shared an hour in common. For example, those relatives who
    meet
in the death chamber of someone deeply loved. In that
    moment
one is lost in her memory, another in his. Their words cross
    each
other unawares. Their hands miss each other in the initial
    confusion.
Until behind them the pain unfurls. They sit, incline their
    brows and
keep silent. Over them a rustling like a forest. They are close
    to one another,
as never before.

XX

Or else, when there is no deep pain to make people
equally silent, one hears more, the other less, of the
    background's
powerful melody. Many never hear it at all. They are like trees
which have forgotten their roots and now think that their
    strength
and life force is the rustling of their branches. Many do not
    have
time to listen. They do not wish for an hour to enclose them.
    These
are the poor homeless ones who have lost the purpose of
    existence.
They strike the keyboard of days and play the same
    monotonous
diminishing note over and over.

XXI

If then we wish to be the initiates of life, we must consider
two things.
First the great melody, in which objects and scents, pasts,
twilights and nostalgia, work together –
and second: the individual voices, that consummate and
accentuate the fullness of this choir.
And for a work of art that means: an image of the deeper life,
of existence that is not only of today, but always possible in all
times, to place in perfect equilibrium the two voices, *that* of the
lasting hour and *that* of the group of people who are reconciled
within it.

XXII

To this end, you must distinguish the two elements of this
   melody
of life in their primitive form; you must extract the rhythm of
   the
waves' sound from the roaring tumult of the sea and from the
tangled net of everyday conversation, somehow draw the one
living line that bears the rest. You must place the pure colours
   side
by side to come to know their contrasts and affinities. You must
have forgotten the many, for the sake of the most important.

XXIII

Two people, who are quiet to an equal degree, they should not
converse about the melody of their hours. This melody is for
    them
the element they have in common. Like a burning altar it
    stands
between them and they feed the holy flame ardently, with their
scattering of syllables.
Now if I place these two people onto a stage, and artistically
    draw
from their being, I do so with the intention of showing two
    lovers
and explaining why they are so blessed. But in the scene, the
    altar
is invisible and none can comprehend the gestures of sacrifice
they are making.

XXIV

There are two ways out of this:
Either the two must stand up and try to state,
with many words and muddled gestures
what they were living before.
Or:
I change nothing in their deepest action
and add these words myself:
Here is an altar on which a sacred flame
burns. You become aware of its light
radiating off the faces of these two people.

XXV

The latter option seems to me the only artistic
one. Nothing of the essential is lost; no confusion
of the simple elements can disturb the course of
events, as long as I depict the altar that unifies
these two solitaries in a way that all see and
believe in its presence. Much later, spectators
will arrive instinctively to observe the fiery column,
and I won't need to add further explanation.
But much later.

XXVI

But this story of the altar is only a parable, and
a vague one at that. What is significant here is
to express on stage their common hour, within
which the two figures come to speak. This song, which
in life is confined to the thousand voices of day or night,
to the rustling of the forest or the ticking of a clock, its
hesitant tolling of the hour, this broad chorus of the
background which determines the rhythm and the tone
of our words, cannot, for the moment, be understood
by such means.

XXVII

For what people call 'atmosphere', that hardly
does itself justice in recent plays – is really just
an initial imperfect attempt to let the landscape
behind the people shimmer through. Most are not
even aware of it, and due to its gentle intimacy
it will never be possible for all to become aware.
Technical amplification of sound or lighting
effects would be absurd, for from a thousand
voices only one rises to a point, so that all action
is left hanging from its edge.

XXVIII

This justice towards the broad song of the background
is only secured if it is valid in wholeness, which for the
moment seems unrealisable, not only due to the means
of our stagecraft, but equally the mistrust of the theatre going
masses. Equilibrium can only be achieved through a rigorous
means of stylisation. Namely, when you play the melody of
    infinity
on the same keyboard on which the hands of the scenic action
    are
placed, it means the great and the wordless are tuned down
to the words.

XXIX

This is nothing more than the implementation of the chorus,
which unfolds calmly behind the light and glimmering
  dialogues.
The silence ceaselessly acting in all its amplitude and
  significance
makes the words in front appear like natural complements, and
  we
can hence envisage a global representation of the song of life,
which, otherwise, seems impossible, since those scents and dark
sensations cannot be employed on stage.

XXX

I wish to refer to a little example:
Evening. A small room. At the central table
two children opposite each other beneath the lamp,
grudgingly bent over their books. They are both
far away – far. The books conceal their flight.
From time to time, they call to each other, so
they won't lose themselves in the vast forest
of their dreams. In this confined space, they
live out fantastic colourful destinies. They fight
and they prevail. They return home and marry.
Teach their children to be heroes. Even die.
I am individual enough to swallow that as a
storyline!

XXXI

But what is this scene without the singing of the
old outmoded hanging lamp, without the breathing
and groaning of the furniture, without the storm
around the house. Without this whole dark background,
through which the children draw the threads of their
fables. How differently these children would dream
in the garden, differently again by the sea, differently
again on a palace terrace. It is not the same thing to
embroider on silk and on wool. People must know
that on the yellow canvas of that evening room, the
pair are reproducing, vaguely, the two clumsy lines
of their meandering pattern.

XXXII

What I propose then, is to let the whole melody
ring out just as the boys hear it. A silent voice
must hover over the scene and at an invisible sign
the tiny voices of the children settle and drift, whilst
the wider current roars on through the narrow
evening room, from infinity to infinity.

XXXIII

I know many such scenes, and still wider ones.
Whether the scene is an explicit, expressly stylised
or more prudent allusion, the chorus will either
find its place in the scene itself and will assert itself
by a vigilant presence, or else it will be reduced to
a voice, which ascends, expanding and impersonal
from the brewing of the common hour. In each
case there resides in this voice, as in the classical
chorus, a wiser knowledge; not because it judges the
events of the storyline, but because it is the foundation
from where this gentle song is released and into whose
lap it finally beautifully falls.

XXXIV

With stylised presentation, in other words, unrealistic,
I see only transition, for the art that we welcome
involuntarily to the scene, is that which resembles life
and which, in this exterior sense is 'true'. Precisely this
approach is the way which leads to a deepening interior
truth: to recognise the primitive elements and employ
them. With solemn experience we will learn to use these
fundamental motifs in a freer and less conventional manner
and at the same time draw closer again to realism, for a
limited time. But this will not be the same as what went
before.

XXXV

These efforts seem necessary to me, otherwise the
knowledge of the most subtle feelings which are acquired
from prolonged and serious work, will be lost in the noise
of the scene as never before. And that would be a shame.
After the scene one could, if it is done without leaning too
heavily towards the tendentious, announce new life, that
is to say communicate equally to those who have not
learned the gestures by their own impulse or strength.
Not that one can convert them due to the scene. But at
least they should experience: that this exists in our epoch,
and so close, surely that is happiness enough.

XXXVI

It is of almost religious significance, this understanding: that
once you have discovered the melody of the background, you
are no longer helpless in your words and confused in your
    decisions.
A serene certitude is born from the simple conviction
that you are part of a melody, that you justifiably hold a certain
place and have a particular task at the heart of a wider work
where all is of equal value, the smallest or greatest.
Not to be excessive is the prime condition for a calm and
conscious unfolding.

XXXVII

All discord and error comes when people seek to find
their element *in* themselves, instead of seeking it *behind*
them, in the light, in landscape at the beginning and in death.
In so doing, they lose themselves and gain nothing in return.
They mingle with each other because they cannot properly
unify. They hold fast to one another and cannot find their feet
since both are unsteady and weak; and in this desire to hold
one another up, they exhaust all their strength, to the extent
that from the outside, they cannot perceive the tangible sound
of a wave.

XXXVIII

But each common element presupposes a series of distinct
solitary beings. Before them, there was a whole denuded of
relationships, existing only for itself. It was neither poor nor
    rich.
From the moment when certain of its parts became alienated
from the maternal unity, it entered into opposition with them,
for in distancing themselves they evolved. But it never lets
go of their hand. Even when the root is ignorant of the fruits,
it nourishes them nevertheless.

XXXIX

And like fruits we are. We hang high on strangely contorted
branches and endure many winds. What is ours is ripeness, our
sweetness and our beauty. But the strength for that runs
    through
the *one* trunk, from a root that widens to cover all. And if we
    want
to witness its power, we have to use it, all of us, in the most
consummate notion of solitude. The more solitary a person is,
the more serious, moving and powerful their community.

XL

And it's rightfully the most solitary beings who possess the
    lion's
share of the community. I stated earlier, that one person
    perceives
more, another less, of the broad melody of life; and
correspondingly each is awarded a greater or lesser
position in the grand orchestra. Whosoever perceives the
melody as a whole will be at once the most solitary and most
deeply embedded in the community. For he will hear what no
    one
else hears, and for this sole reason will understand in his
consummation, what the rest catch as incomplete fragments.

Appendix I:
Rilke's Residencies in Paris 1902–25

11 rue Toullier
August – October 1902

3 rue l'Abbé-de l'Epée
October 1902 – March 1903
May – June 1903

Hôtel du Quai Voltaire
11–15 September 1905
31 May – 5 June 1907

Meudon – House of Rodin
15 September 1905 – 12 May 1906

29 rue Cassette
May – July 1906
6 June – 31 October 1907

Hôtel Biron, 77 rue de Varenne
1 September 1908 – May 1909
31 May – August 1909
September 1909
9 October 1909 – 11 January 1910
14 May 1910 – 8 July 1910
1 November–18 November 1910
6 April – July 1911
26 September – October 1911

17 rue Campagne-Première

2 May – 31 August 1908

27 February – June 1913

20 October 1913 – 25 February 1914

21 March – April 1914

26 May – July 1914

Hôtel Foyot, 33 rue Tournon

21–28 October 1920

6 January – August 1925

Appendix II
A Note on the Original Edition of
Rilke in Paris

The principal publisher Maurice Betz used for his Rilke translations was Emile-Paul Frères, based at 14 rue de l'Abbaye in the 6th arrondissement of Paris, who today no longer exist. Betz had already published a number of Rilke related books with Emile-Paul, most notably *Rilke Vivant: Souvenirs, lettres, entretiens* in 1937, so it seemed logical that it was they who published in the summer of 1941, in a handsome collectable edition, Betz's essay on Rilke's relationship with Paris, which focused on the now famous *Cahiers* Betz himself had translated. *Rilke à Paris* appeared at the lowest point in the Second World War, a year into France's occupation, and one can only wonder at its reception and who of literary note was even left in Paris to register its arrival. Betz's book must have seemed rather out of place, like a genteel throwback to another age, which appeared, due to the depraved realities of the ongoing European catastrophe, to have been shunted even further back into history than a mere handful of decades. For Betz, *Rilke à Paris* was a summing up of his reflections on Rilke, both a tribute and a farewell. Betz survived the war, but died in 1946. The year preceding his death, Emile-Paul Frères published, in honour of their translator, an attractive pamphlet edition of Rilke's *Fragments sur la Guerre*, mainly extracts from letters to various friends on his first impressions of the conflict, using the same book design motif as for *Rilke à Paris*.

The first edition of *Rilke à Paris* was limited to a hundred numbered copies and appeared on 14 July 1941. The book was reborn some sixty years later in truncated form, when modern French publisher Obsidiane reissued a facsimile copy of the original in the year 2000. However this edition lacked the impact and imposing aesthetic of the original, and appeared something of a rushed job by a clearly cash-strapped publisher. The original photographs were intact but were poorly reproduced. There was no new introduction putting the work in context, and interesting supplementary texts in the original had strangely been omitted, from the facsimile, including the important list of Rilke's Paris addresses. One of the things the original edition included as examples of letters, now well known, that Rilke had written to various persons, but principally to his wife Clara, giving those first visceral impressions of Paris. Betz presented these with the equivalent sections of the *Notebooks*, in order to show how close the letters were to the final draft of the prose work. I include one of these excerpts at the beginning of the English translation. 'Ah, the achievement of a young moon…' Anyone who has access to Rilke's letters can see that this and other sections of the *Notebooks* are culled almost verbatim from letters written at the time, mostly to Clara. For Rilke his letters were often prose works in their own right, either prefiguring a work to come or allowing their author to set out in writing his most pressing thoughts before they dispersed, and either to encourage a response from a recipient or just to leave a record. It is evident when reading Rilke's letters that often they lose track completely of the person they are addressed to and one senses time and again that these letters are mere springboards for an articulation of some sensory development, which is best served by the undemanding non pre-scriptive structure of a letter. Betz also included a fascinating list of Rilke's addresses during the course of his various sojourns in the French capital, which I have reproduced here. Many of these buildings are still intact and the streets little changed, at least in their physical dimensions. At 29 rue Cassette for example, the wall opposite his apartment separating rue Cassette from the church, which Rilke mentions in the *Notebooks*, and which Betz highlights in an excerpt, is still there.

Rilke's residences are located at various positions close to the Luxembourg Gardens, like so many satellites revolving around that most cherished space for contemplation. It seems Rilke never departed from the Left Bank, even the Hotel Quai Voltaire overlooking the Louvre across the Seine, was at its very limit. The most relevant to Betz's essay are Rilke's first lodgings in rue Toullier in the 5th and rue Cassette in the 6th arrondissements. But the most frequented of the addresses and the only place where Rilke really felt a semblance of repose and settlement, was the then under-appreciated romantically faded Hôtel Biron, which sheltered him in the period 1909–1911. The other long-standing abode was at 17 rue Campagne-Première in Montparnasse, where he was still residing at the outbreak of the First World War and from which he was forced to flee in the summer of 1914, as once fluid national borders began abruptly to solidify.

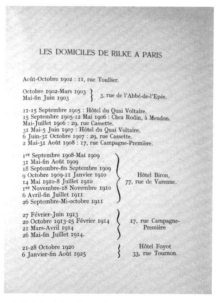

LES DOMICILES DE RILKE A PARIS

Août-Octobre 1902 : 11, rue Toullier.

Octobre 1902-Mars 1903 }
Mai-fin Juin 1903 } 3, rue de l'Abbé-de-l'Epée.

11-15 Septembre 1905 : Hôtel du Quai Voltaire.
15 Septembre 1905-12 Mai 1906 : Chez Rodin, à Meudon.
Mai-Juillet 1906 : 29, rue Cassette.
31 Mai-5 Juin 1907 : Hôtel du Quai Voltaire.
6 Juin-31 Octobre 1907 : 29, rue Cassette.
2 Mai-31 Août 1908 : 17, rue Campagne-Première.

1er Septembre 1908-Mai 1909
31 Mai-fin Août 1909
18 Septembre-fin Septembre 1909
9 Octobre 1909-11 Janvier 1910   Hôtel Biron,
14 Mai 1910-8 Juillet 1910   77, rue de Varenne.
1er Novembre-18 Novembre 1910
6 Avril-fin Juillet 1911
26 Septembre-Mi-octobre 1911

27 Février-Juin 1913
20 Octobre 1913-25 Février 1914   17, rue Campagne-
21 Mars-Avril 1914   Première
26 Mai-fin Juillet 1914.

21-28 Octobre 1920   Hôtel Foyot
6 Janvier-fin Août 1925   33, rue Tournon.

16. Original Emile-Paul Frères edition of
Rilke à Paris, 1941

17. Original Emile-Paul Frères edition of *Rilke à Paris*, 1941.
Rilke, Paris 1925

18. Original Emile-Paul Frères edition of *Rilke à Paris*, 1941.
Rodin, Paris 1904

Appendix III
A Note on Photographs

It was decided to incorporate photographs into the text of *Rilke in Paris* in order to echo the spirit of the original. The French edition displayed a famous photograph of Rodin dating from 1904, an often-reproduced portrait of Rilke from 1925, a facsimile of the text of the *Notebooks* and a period picture of the Hôtel Biron. These images are clearly visible in the photographs of the *Rilke à Paris* original edition reproduced here. For the first English edition there will be new black and white photographs by my own hand, certain of which will echo the original images and others which will, I trust, be sympathetic, even though they were not originally present. These images have been created expressly for this publication and are designed to evoke in some modest way at least the physical remains of the Paris that Rilke was closest to and moved in. My aim throughout has been not only to translate Betz's book to the best of my ability, but to honour its style and aesthetic judgments as best I can, given the unsympathetic modern cultural parameters in which we are obliged to operate.

HESPERUS PRESS

Hesperus Press is committed to bringing near what is far – far both in space and time. Works written by the greatest authors, and unjustly neglected or simply little known in the English-speaking world, are made accessible through new translations and a completely fresh editorial approach. Through these classic works, the reader is introduced to the greatest writers from all times and all cultures.

For more information on Hesperus Press, please visit our website: **www.hesperuspress.com**